# Katie's Hero

## Cody Young

CRIMSON
ROMANCE
Avon, Massachusetts

This edition published by
Crimson Romance
an imprint of F+W Media, Inc.
10151 Carver Road, Suite 200
Blue Ash, Ohio 45242

*www.crimsonromance.com*

# Dedication

THE ROYAL AIR FORCE HAS A MOTTO, "PER ARDUA AD ASTRA," WHICH MEANS "THROUGH STRUGGLE TO THE STARS." I THINK ABOUT THAT MOTTO A LOT WHILE I'M WRITING, ESPECIALLY WHEN I'M WRITING ABOUT LOVE. THIS BOOK IS DEDICATED TO THOSE WHO HAVE STRUGGLED, AND TO THOSE WHO ARE STILL SEARCHING FOR THE RIGHT PERSON TO LOVE.

# Prologue

*October 1940*

The air raid siren wailed and Katie felt another contraction surging.

"You can't drop it here, girl, we've got to get to the shelter!"

Katie felt someone tug at her sleeve, pulling her along, urging her to hurry. As the contraction eased, she opened her eyes and saw her roommate Joan's concerned face.

"I need a doctor!" Katie's water broke and ran down her legs, fluid tinged pink with blood.

Joan looked terrified. "In this? Are you mad! You'll be needing an undertaker if you don't hurry up."

They ran around the corner and into the next street. Ahead they could see a crowd of people all pushing and shoving, hurrying down into the Tube station. A bottleneck was forming by the entrance.

The first bomb hit a few streets away, and the girls were buffeted several feet along the road, like a couple of pieces of litter picked up by the wind.

"For the baby's sake, get me to a doctor," begged Katie.

"We'll see about getting one when the raid's over," Joan said. "Babies take ages."

"Are you sure about that? Oh . . . Holy Mary, Mother of God . . . " Katie said, hoping the familiar words would chase away her pain. A man with a briefcase held over his head nearly knocked Katie off her feet, fighting to get past her, jostling to get to the entrance.

"Silly Irish cow," the young man said. "Get out of the way!"

Joan was angry. "She's having a baby, Mister. You could help her, if you had an ounce of humanity in you!"

But he disappeared down into the shelter along with everyone else.

Katie couldn't move. She couldn't think about anything except the ferocious pain that held her in its grip. "Joan, go! You get down the stairs now, I'll follow."

Another blast. Much closer. The roof tiles on the houses just opposite the Tube station cascaded like dominoes into the street. They seemed to fall onto the pavement in silence. Their sound could not compete with the deafening bombs.

Katie gripped her belly and gave a moan. She looked at poor, terrified Joan and tried to yell, "Go!" but she wasn't sure if she'd managed to utter a sound.

Joan took one last, guilty look at Katie and ran down the steps into the shelter.

The building across the road began to crumble away before Katie's eyes. The bricks came tumbling down—again effortlessly, silently—as the whole front wall peeled away and toppled to the ground.

"Now and at the hour of our death . . . " she said softly, but she couldn't hear the words.

Then Katie felt a man's arm around her, and she was lifted up and carried down the steps at the same moment a river of bricks rolled toward the entrance to the underground station. Katie buried her face against the gray cloth of his RAF jacket and refused to admit that she was lucky to be alive. She didn't feel lucky at all.

He carried her down to the shelter, where the crowd quickly surrounded Katie, some from concern, others for the distraction. It wasn't every day a girl went into labor in the middle of an air raid.

A woman leaned forward and spoke to Katie. "What a time to choose, luv!"

"I didn't choose. It was Hitler," Katie said.

No pain relief, no bed, no hot water, and no doctor. Not a good way to bring a little person into the world, and Katie desperately wished she could have done better. Even if the child should never have been born, it deserved far better than this.

"Where shall I put her?" the man in the RAF uniform asked.

"Over here," a woman called out, "I've had six of me own. I'll do what I can for her."

As the man laid her down gently on a blanket, Katie looked up and saw his face for the first time. A hero's face, lean and young. Concerned blue eyes, gazing down at her. He wore the peaked gray cap of an officer. Leagues above me, she thought, and yet he stopped to help. Her fingers touched the wings emblem on his jacket.

"You're a pilot?"

"Yes," he said, with a devastating smile. "Fighters," he added, with a note of pride. She was still cradled in his arms when the next contraction came. She moaned and gave herself up to the pain. When it passed, she realized how tightly she gripped his hand.

He gazed down at her, eyes full of compassion. "Brave girl," he said, in a voice that spoke of public schools and old money.

Katie sighed. She didn't feel brave.

"I'm afraid I have to leave you now," he said, apologetically. "I'm on a forty-eight hour pass, and I reckon I'm up to about forty-nine already!"

The woman next to Katie laughed. "You ain't going nowhere tonight, handsome. Not now. The way out's blocked. They'll have to dig us out in the morning."

The young pilot looked up. "I'd like to stay, but duty calls." He looked down at Katie one last time and squeezed her hand. "Good luck," he said, instead of goodbye.

He moved to the edge of the platform, and in one athletic leap, vaulted down onto the tracks to the astonishment and disapproval of about two hundred Londoners. He ran across the railway line and leaped up onto the other side. There he ran up the steps, two at a time, and disappeared in the direction of the exit.

The woman shrugged and turned back to Katie.

"Where you from, luv?"

"County Clare."

"Should've stayed there. Much more peaceful."

Katie's face contorted, and someone wiped her brow with a damp rag—another woman with a kinder face. "Nearly over now. Soon be done."

"Too soon," Katie said, fretting about the outcome. If only she hadn't run when the siren sounded. If only she'd been more careful. Months ago, she should have been more careful. Or he should. Tom, back in Ireland. She should have known better. She swore she'd never look at a man again, not like that—it only led to pain and heartache like this. She gave a long, desperate howl.

"Hush, luv. Can't be helped."

# Chapter One

The trained steamed in to the station, and Katie alighted at the tiny platform in what seemed to be the middle of nowhere. She was thankful to have left London. It made it easier to forget.

The train pulled out of the station, and once the hiss, steam and smoke had subsided, it was very quiet. Katie was entirely alone for a few minutes, until an enormous woman in a dark blue uniform appeared from the back of the tiny ticket office.

The woman stuck out a hand for Katie to shake. "Marjory Mallory," she said in a hearty voice, "of the WRVS."

Here was a flagship for the Women's Royal Voluntary Service if ever there was one, thought Katie, and smiled. "Katie Rafferty, of nowhere in particular."

"I'll take you up to his lordship's house," Mrs. Mallory said, sounding important and authoritative. "We must walk, to save petrol and be patriotic."

At first, they walked along in silence. Katie was glad that Mrs. Mallory didn't require her to talk, as she preferred the quiet rhythm of their footsteps on the country lane. Every step was taking her further away from London, and that was all that mattered. For now.

It was cold, Katie's suitcase was heavy, and there was no sign of a house up ahead, only a deep-cut lane shadowed by trees. It was wet underfoot and her shoes weren't keeping the water out. Katie wasn't sure it was patriotic to wear out such a lot of shoe leather, but she was in no position to argue—she was relying on Mrs. Mallory to find her a safe place to spend the rest of the war. Safe and *warm*, would be lovely, but Katie knew that posh houses weren't very cozy, generally speaking, so she wasn't getting her hopes up.

It had sounded like a good offer, when she got the letter. She was to look after four children, evacuees from London, in a lovely old house owned by a lord, no less. It would be easy work, the letter assured her, and it was situated in the depths of the countryside in Hertfordshire, so it would be much safer than being in a big city that might be bombed at any moment.

"You like children?" Mrs. Mallory asked, gently. Breaking the silence.

Katie nodded. She loved children, and being the oldest of a rowdy family of ten this was a love born of experience, not just a notion.

The older woman took that as her cue to tell Katie more about her new place, and how lucky she was to have found it. But the more Mrs. Mallory told her, the more worried Katie became. She went pale when she heard that the children wouldn't be arriving until Friday.

"He doesn't live alone, does he?" Katie said in alarm.

"He has a housekeeper, dear, but she doesn't live in."

"But . . . *I'm* living in, and I'm to stay there, tonight, with him?" As soon as the words were out, Katie knew that she'd sounded like a silly Irish girl, afraid to spend the night under the same roof as a man she didn't know and wasn't sure if she could trust.

"Michael is a gentleman," Mrs. Mallory said, in her deep, plummy voice. She gave a short, sad sigh. "He was such a nice boy—before the war."

Katie stopped for a moment, setting the suitcase down. The handle was cutting into her hand, hurting her. "Sorry," she murmured apologetically.

"Let me," Mrs. Mallory insisted. "You've been struggling with that for nearly a mile. I'll take it the rest of the way." She grabbed the case in her strong right hand and set off at a fast clip.

Katie tried to protest. Mrs. Mallory was definitely a member of what some people called "the better sort." It didn't seem right for her to be carrying the suitcase. Katie would rather have carried it until her fingers bled than endure the embarrassment of seeming like a girl who didn't know her place. Still, Mrs. Mallory insisted.

"Not far now. No need to be a martyr!"

Katie smiled weakly. Sometimes, when the tanks roll in, you just had to stand back and watch.

"There are one or two things you've got to understand about Michael, my dear." Mrs. Mallory paused, as if she didn't know how to broach the next bit. "You see, poor Michael—I refuse to call him Lord Farrenden; I've known him since he was a little boy and he's only twenty-six now. Anyway, Michael was flying sorties and participating in dogfights—he was a wonderful pilot, by all accounts—when his plane caught fire and . . . "

"Oh, ma'am, is he terribly disfigured?" Katie was getting more and more frightened, imagining the worst. Her new employer was a man living alone, which was bad enough. Now, in her mind's eye, he was some kind of gargoyle, a fearsome sight, ranting incoherently and roaming the corridors of his posh house. On the lookout for young Irish girls, no doubt.

Mrs. Mallory actually laughed at that. "No! He bailed out. He was injured, though, and he won't fly again. He's bitter. War does that to people. I'm old enough to have seen it all before, but that would have been before you were born. I should think you're a bit too young to understand."

At nineteen, Katie certainly didn't feel young after everything that had happened to her during the last year, but she bit her tongue. Older people always thought they knew it all already. Or else they must have forgotten all the pain involved in being young, or they wouldn't hate young people so much for something that they couldn't do anything about. That was Katie's theory, anyway.

"He can't go on rattling around in his empty house mourning the dead," said Mrs. Mallory, "when we've got a trainload of youngsters to find places for by Friday. Everyone else in the village has been approached. Michael can't pull rank and refuse to help when he has so much and the rest of us have so little. I went in there and had a stern talk with him last week. He only agreed to it when

I said I'd find him a girl to help out. He's only got Mrs. Jessop, now. She comes in to do a bit of cooking and cleaning for him, but she's nearly seventy if she's a day. You'll need to pitch in with the work."

Katie nodded. She didn't mind hard work at all, as long as there was a warm kitchen, regular meals and a safe place to sleep at night.

"How do you get on with boys, Katie?"

"I . . . I beg your pardon?" Katie knew she had begun to blush.

"Boys. Farrenden Manor seemed the ideal place to send boys. So I'm afraid you're getting a small horde of them. I thought they could run about on the lawn or work off their energy in the woods. There's good fishing in that river, as long as they've got some supervision, or swimming in the lake if the war isn't over by next summer."

"That sort of boys, ma'am. No problem at all," Katie said.

"Excellent. Excellent," Mrs. Mallory said. "But don't take any nonsense from them, dear. I've had the village hall full of these kids before, and some of them were right little devils. I had to find billets for them all, so I know exactly what to expect. This lot are Londoners, too, so you'll have to keep a close eye on them."

Katie nodded.

Finally and suddenly, the house, grand and imposing, stood in the clearing in front of the two travelers. It was breathtaking, a lovely place made of pale gray stone. It was an elegant building with tall windows. Three stories high, with a huge double door, approached by an imposing set of stone steps.

"Oh, but it's beautiful!" Katie said, indulging in a good long look. "Imagine me, working in a place like that! It's like a pale gray version of the White House, Mrs. Mallory. Not that I've ever seen the White House, of course, only in picture books and the like. But isn't it grand!"

"All of a sudden you sound so very Irish, my dear," Mrs. Mallory said, but her face creased into a smile, so Katie knew she didn't mean it unkindly.

Still, Katie was quite alarmed when the indomitable Mrs. Mallory started marching up the stone steps leading to the great front door.

"I'd feel a lot more comfortable if we went around the back, Mrs. Mallory," Katie said, and tugged at the older woman's sleeve. "I'm the hired help."

"Yes, dear, but I am not, and in all the years I have known the Farrenden family, I have never yet felt so much in awe of them that I couldn't use the front door."

She rang the bell.

There was no sign of life from inside the house. Mrs. Mallory frowned.

"I do hope Lizzie Jessop hasn't gone home. There's no butler now, more's the pity. A door like this deserves a butler, doesn't it?"

"His lordship wouldn't come to the door himself?" Katie asked in an anxious murmur.

"Not bloody likely," the older woman said, "but he'll want to have a look at you, no doubt."

Katie gulped and glanced down at the scuffed toes of her soaking wet shoes. Instinctively, her hand moved to touch the place where her jacket was missing a button. She fought the urge to tidy her hair in case someone opened the door while she was in the middle of combing it. She knew her auburn curls would be in total disarray. Her heart stuttered when Mrs. Mallory rang the bell for the third time, and it seemed to stop altogether when a stern old woman with gray hair opened the door.

She wore her hair nineteen-thirties style, in a low bun on the nape of her neck. She was a bit of a hatchet-faced thing, and she wore a floral pinafore over her winter skirt and blouse. Mrs. Mallory addressed her as Lizzie, though she seemed far too starchy for a name like that, and Katie got the feeling that "Mrs. Jessop"— murmured in a submissive, deferential tone—would be the very least that was expected from *her*.

The housekeeper turned and studied Katie, giving her one of those up and down appraisals that people sometimes got at difficult job interviews, though Katie had been given to understand that the job was hers if she wanted it.

The housekeeper didn't seem entirely happy with Katie, but she kept her criticisms to herself. "I'll let him know you're here," she said instead.

She crossed the great square hall with its checkered tiles, and Katie and Mrs. Mallory followed respectfully in her wake.

The old lady knocked at the door of his lordship's study.

"Come!" he called.

He had a commanding voice, Katie thought, a posh bloke's voice. The housekeeper went in and crossed the room, but Mrs. Mallory didn't follow her, so Katie stayed where she was. Peering through the ajar door, Katie was curious to catch a glimpse of her new employer. He was seated at his desk near the fireplace, with his back to her. His hair was fair, and shone gold in the firelight. He looked up to speak to his housekeeper and in profile he had an aristocratic face, with a long Roman nose—the kind that went with the commanding voice—though he looked a little more boyish than she had expected. He wore a gray civilian jacket, very nicely tailored. He was rather slim, from what she could see, and there was no sign at all of an injury or a war wound.

"About bloody time," she heard him say, "the train must have drawn in at the station over an hour ago."

Katie tensed. There was something familiar about his voice.

The housekeeper was apologetic. "They walked, your lordship."

"They should have been met, Jessop. Why didn't you organize that?"

"I didn't think it my place, sir, to make that decision . . . "

"Not your place! Have you no common sense, woman!"

He's dreadful, thought Katie. For a man with quite a pleasing appearance, he had the most horribly arrogant and high-handed manner with his housekeeper. He was obviously in the wrong, too. He should have issued proper instructions if he wanted things done a certain way. If his long-time, faithful servant had to put up with that kind of tongue-lashing, what chance was there for her? Katie knew she'd never please him in a thousand years. Mrs. Jessop beckoned them forward, and Katie took a last look at Mrs. Mallory for solidarity before entering the dragon's lair.

"Try to smile, dear," Mrs. Mallory whispered, "I promised him I'd find him someone pretty!"

\*

Michael maneuvered his wheelchair with expert skill. He backed it up about half a yard and then spun it around to face his visitors. He jerked his head up to look at them. He hated having to look *up* at people all the time. It was demeaning for a man who had stood at six foot two, last time he was able to stand. It was as if *they* were very important and he was kneeling at their feet.

"Michael, dear! You look awful," Mrs. Mallory said.

Michael knew he'd become thinner and paler since the accident, but he had checked his reflection in the mirror just fifteen minutes ago and thought he still had the face of a handsome young flier.

"Thank you so much," he said in a sour tone, as Mrs. Mallory plonked the suitcase down beside his chair and leaned forward to give him an unwelcome kiss.

"No roses in your cheeks," she said, pinching them with her fingers as if she could improve them, while Michael shrank back in his chair in disgust.

"Marjory—"

"And you always look so cross!"

Michael rolled his eyes in annoyance. Mrs. Mallory always treated him as if he was a small boy. She started asking him some rubbish about the house, but he didn't hear the details because he was too busy staring at the girl. She looked frightened out of her wits. She was very pale, with wide, dark eyes that did nothing to hide her fear. Mrs. Mallory obviously hadn't warned her about the bloody wheelchair, because she was staring at it as if it might burst into flames, or start careening toward her like Boadicea's chariot. He gave a little snort of amusement. His hands stayed firmly on the wheels to keep it in place. Some things, at least, were completely under his control.

"Miss Rafferty?"

"Very pleased to meet you, Mr . . . my lord . . . ship," she said uncertainly.

That amused him a little, too. "Have you come all the way from Ireland, today?" he asked. He didn't care if he sounded laconic. Lords were allowed to be laconic.

She looked at her feet, and a strand of curly auburn hair fell in front of her face. "No, sir. From London, sir."

"Have we met before? At a dance, or something?"

"No, sir. I don't believe we have," she replied.

He didn't think he was mistaken, but he didn't challenge her. He noticed the missing button on her little tweed suit, and the way she tried to conceal it with her left hand. He noticed her hands, too. Lily white and very shapely. He suspected her ankles were shapely too, though it was hard to tell because she was wearing such awful, wrinkly stockings.

"The place she was staying was bombed out, Michael," Mrs. Mallory explained, since it was clear that Katie was keeping her responses as minimal as she dared. "Katie has been living in a Tube station, according to my sister-in-law. She needs alternative accommodation, and we need her help. So here she is."

"Indeed she is." Michael appraised her once more. She was still almost quaking with fear, he realized. Surely she was over the initial shock of the meeting a cripple by now? "Why on earth did you leave Ireland, Miss Rafferty? Why didn't you stay where there isn't a war?"

"For heaven's sake, Michael, where are your manners?" Mrs. Mallory scolded. "We need a hot drink, if not something stronger, and Katie needs to know where she will be sleeping."

"The attic would be absolutely fine," Katie announced, a little too fast.

Michael raised an eyebrow.

Katie gave a nervous laugh. "Then I won't be disturbing anyone with my Hail Marys." She turned to Mrs. Mallory, as if she was silently asking for her help.

"Miss Rafferty is very anxious not to get under your feet," the older woman explained, "until the children arrive on Friday."

"I see," Michael said, though he wasn't sure that he *did* see.

"She comes from a very respectable family, Michael, and she is very young."

"I can see that. I almost thought she was one of the bloody evacuees when she first arrived." Michael noticed that Katie colored up a little at his blunt remark.

"Yes, she's young and far from home," Mrs. Mallory said, "and she hasn't worked for anyone but her own mother before, helping out with her brothers and sisters. So, she needs to know that you wouldn't compromise her in any way, Michael."

Michael stared back in disbelief, but apparently Mrs. Mallory was quite serious. Her face didn't flinch. She was a marvelous ambassador for the WRVS, with her unbreakable spirit and her undentable hat, but she was a real pain in the neck as far as Michael was concerned. She sat, stately and imposing in her enormous dark blue uniform, waiting for his reply.

Michael felt a flash of anger. "How very kind you are, Marjory," he said in a hostile voice. "How amusing to suggest that I might be able to compromise a woman, now that I'm stuck in this thing."

*

Katie knew her face was scarlet with embarrassment. Surely this wasn't the way it was meant to go when a girl met her new employer. If that's how he spoke to Mrs. Mallory, she dreaded what he might say to her next. She hoped, desperately, that he wouldn't ask her any more questions about where they had met before. She couldn't—

she wouldn't—think about that night. Then Mrs. Jessop came in with a tray of tea, although she hadn't been summoned.

Mrs. Mallory clapped her hands in delight. "Look Katie, there's a lovely fruitcake, too! Now isn't that a welcome sight after all the shortages in London?" Mrs. Mallory removed her hat as if to indicate that a more relaxed mood would be appreciated. She reached for the teapot. "Shall I be mother?"

Katie tried to slow her breathing down to a normal rhythm. She received her cup of tea carefully, hoping that his lordship didn't notice that the cup jingled against the saucer as she lifted it up to take a sip. She tried the fruitcake too, and found that there wasn't really any fruit in it at all. It was dust and ashes. She was a little surprised—she had been led to believe that people ate better in the country, and Farrenden Estate was a working farm, for goodness sake.

Like a curious schoolboy, Michael reached out and picked up Mrs. Mallory's hat. Katie watched him as he turned it around in his long, slim hands, admiring it from every angle. He rapped the top of it with his knuckles, and it made an audible "knock, knock" sound.

"Thought so," he said.

Mrs. Mallory snatched it back. "Michael, don't spoil that. I'd have a devil of a job getting them to issue me a replacement."

Katie smiled. She relaxed enough to look around the room. It was big and square, with a high ceiling. Bookshelves lined one wall, and Michael's antique desk stood over on one side. A pair of tall, double doors had been left open beyond the desk, and she could see through to the next room. There was a bed in there, and she realized it must be where his lordship slept, though it had obviously been a drawing room or billiard room before. It looked as if a hand basin had been installed in there, too. It must have been an inconvenience to him, reorganizing his entire life around his disability.

As if he saw where she was looking, Michael spoke up sharply. "The children are not to run amok in my private chambers. They are to be kept quiet at all times, Miss Rafferty. This is my study, as you see, and from here, I run the estate. I expect complete acquiescence to my wishes and to my rules. I have written them down in a list, if you will care to familiarize yourself with them."

He reached into the inside of his jacket pocket and fetched out a piece of foolscap, folded into four, to hand to Katie.

She unfolded it, gingerly. It was handwritten in black ink, in a stern hand: The children are not allowed to play games in the hall, on the stairs or along the balcony. Sliding down the banisters is strictly forbidden. The children are to remain quiet and respectful at all times. The children must use the kitchen door when coming and going from school. Homework must be completed before supper, or supper and other privileges will be withdrawn.

Katie could only conclude that Michael hadn't encountered many children in the first twenty-six years of his life.

After tea, Mrs. Jessop finally showed Katie to her room, which she was careful to praise to the older woman. There was a narrow bed with a navy blue coverlet, and a little table with a tiny lamp. The floorboards were dark, covered with a rug made of braided strips of fabric beside the bed. There was a mirror, thank goodness. But the curtains were a bit musty, and there didn't seem to be anywhere for Katie to hang her clothes, except for one peg on the back of the door. When she sat down on the edge of the bed it didn't give at all—a concrete slab would have had more bounce. The room was a bit depressing after the grandeur of the rest of the house, but it was a vast improvement on a London Underground Station.

Mrs. Jessop announced it was time for her to head home, and so it was Katie who showed Mrs. Mallory to the door.

The older woman hesitated before setting off for the long walk back to the village. "I hope you'll be happy here, dear, and that your first impressions of Michael aren't too bad."

"Oh ma'am, he hates himself and everyone else in the world," Katie said, keeping her voice low in case he was listening.

"He's been through a lot," Mrs. Mallory said. "The accident changed him out of all recognition."

"Why doesn't he have a nurse?"

"He did, when he first came home, but she was a bit of a tartar, and as soon as he could manage on his own, he sacked the old trout. He barely tolerates Jessop. You concentrate on getting into his good books, dear. It will do him good to have someone young in the house. Goodbye, and good luck."

Katie sighed. A bitter, broken man for an employer. A musty room with a concrete bed. A list of rules to memorize before Friday.

Worse than that. Much worse, was the unspoken connection between her and Michael Farrenden. She needed to forget that terrible night in the Tube station. She wanted to start afresh. She'd hoped—desperately—never to have to think about that time again. But she had seen that flicker of recognition on his face. And it forced memories back into her mind that she would much rather forget.

Oh God, yes, she remembered. She remembered the pain, and the fear, and the feel of his RAF jacket against her face. She remembered squeezing his hand, and his telling her she was a brave girl. She remembered the athletic way he had disappeared from her life, forever, she had assumed.

Katie consoled herself with the thought that she didn't have to speak to him again until tomorrow, when they would discuss the arrangements for the children. Her room was not in the attic, but at least it was upstairs, and having those stairs between her and Michael Farrenden gave her a great feeling of security.

A man in a wheelchair couldn't climb stairs, she presumed.

The last thing she did before going to bed was to re-read Tom's latest letter. Tom O'Brien, who danced so well, talked so well, and kissed so well . . . Katie didn't understand why he'd written at all since they had parted on fighting terms. She had told him that she never wanted to see him again in her life. She should burn his letter instead of reading it again, but she didn't.

*To my sweetheart, Katie,*

Damn cheek! Still calling her his sweetheart!

*I am writing to tell you that my father passed away three weeks ago now.*

That had been a shock. Mr. O'Brien from the general store was a tough old boot. Katie didn't think he'd had a day's illness in his life. Mr. O'Brien, dead?

*It was his heart.*

It seemed very unlikely that he had one, Katie thought, remembering the callous way the O'Brien family had treated her when they found out that Tom had got her pregnant.

*So, there've been a few changes here. I've taken over the shop, for one thing, and it's got me thinking about you and me.*

Katie sighed. Here it comes.

*You're a fine girl, and I've been missing you. Why have you not come back to Ireland?*

I told you, Tom. I never want to lay eyes on you again.

*You must have had the child by now. Why have you not come back to take up the threads of your old life?*

Her old life? Katie couldn't believe his insensitivity. He *knew* her mam and her dad had been disappointed when she started carrying on with Tom. They'd had such high hopes for her. He knew that she had lied to them about the nursing job in England, and that they had guessed the reason why. He knew that her sisters had been told never to mention Katie's name in the house again.

*I was wondering if the baby was a boy or a girl? Did he look like me? I suppose you didn't give him my name, did you?*

Katie bit her lip. She didn't want to read any of this anymore.

*Anyway, if you could see your way to coming back, we could put the past behind us. You could help me run the shop. It's a lot of work, but we could be happy. I miss you so much. I think it will all work out just fine.*

Never.

*Love and kisses from Tom.*

Katie gave a sort of gasp as if she couldn't breathe. If he had any idea how she felt about his love and his kisses now! How she cursed the day she met him at the dance at the railway hotel, and how bitterly she wished she had not caught his eye.

There was no fire in the grate in Katie's bedroom, but she lit a candle so she could burn the offensive letter. She took it over near the fireplace, and set light to it there so it wouldn't make too much of a mess. It crumbled into little flakes of blackened ash, and when it was gone, Katie went and lay on the bed and cried herself to sleep.

# Chapter Two

Katie woke early, too jittery to sleep any longer. She dressed in a plain skirt and a hand-knitted twin set. She considered putting on the little string of artificial pearls that Tom had bought for her, but she decided that was too showy for today. She wanted to look capable and efficient. She wanted to look like the type of young woman who could cope with anything this war flung at her. She brushed out her hair, and clipped it up at the sides. She reached for her lipstick. Red—the red badge of courage, people called it—and if ever there were a day when she needed some of that, it was today. She practiced her smile.

"Good morning, your lordship," she repeated aloud until she could say it without faltering or sounding fake. She squared her shoulders and went downstairs.

She headed for the kitchen, where there was no sign of anyone, to her great relief. She made herself a quick breakfast and washed it down with weak tea.

Mrs. Jessop arrived in a headscarf and a large, old-fashioned overcoat. She spent ages taking off her outer garments, placing them on the coat stand and finally donning her floral housecoat.

"How long has his lordship been in a wheelchair?" Katie asked.

"Five months, nearly six." Mrs. Jessop went over to the enormous butler's sink and began washing up Katie's cup and saucer, tutting in disapproval. "He bailed out of his plane. Landed on somebody's roof. Broke his back."

It was brutal sounding, when put like that. Katie shivered. "Poor man," she murmured, though Lord Farrenden was so proud and haughty it hardly seemed right to feel sorry for him.

"That's what everyone calls him these days," Mrs. Jessop observed, in an acid tone of voice. "*Poor man*—as if it was part

22

of his title! You have no idea how he was before. Such a charmer. Loads of girlfriends. The parties he used to hold here—champagne on ice, streamers in the hallway, dancing until four in the morning. He loved dancing. He was good at it, too—along with everything else he did. Flying, shooting, skiing in Switzerland. He could ride a horse better than anyone in the county. Nobody would have called him *poor man* then."

Katie gulped. "No."

Mrs. Jessop shook her head. "Now look at him. Sits in his study. Doesn't want to go anywhere. Doesn't want to see anyone. Doesn't want to be disturbed."

"Perhaps when the children arrive . . . " Katie began.

"He's not used to youngsters. He was an only child."

Katie's heart sank.

Mrs. Jessop began preparing a breakfast tray for Michael. A boiled egg, some rounds of toast, kept warm under a shiny metal lid. The cutlery was real silver, buffed up on a polishing cloth. Jessop arranged the butter knife reverentially and laid a clean white napkin beside it. She put a tiny quantity of marmalade in a cut glass dish and placed a camellia flower beside it.

"Is there something I can help with?" Katie asked.

"No. I doubt you would have any idea how a gentleman likes things done. Amuse yourself while I take this to his lordship and help him dress. Lunch will be at twelve, and this afternoon we'll make the necessary preparations for the children." Mrs. Jessop pursed her lips.

Clearly, Mrs. Jessop wasn't looking forward to the evacuees' arrival.

Katie gave a mute, obedient nod.

Then Mrs. Jessop picked up the tray and disappeared in the direction of his lordship's rooms.

*A whole morning of freedom*, thought Katie, and she was on her feet the instant the old woman was out of the way.

She hurried upstairs and dashed off a dutiful, distant letter to her parents, telling them she was well looked after and settling in— just to salve her conscience. It was only fair to let them know she had a new place to stay. She grabbed her hat and coat and decided to walk down to the village to put it in the post straight away. But she'd longed for a chance to explore the house, and knowing that Mrs. Jessop and his lordship were out of the way made wandering the halls all the more tempting.

Katie slipped down the corridor that led to the front of the house and walked quietly across the checkered floor of the entrance hall.

She opened the first door she came to, a well-appointed reception room with a view across the drive. She moved to stand by the huge fireplace and stared up at the massive oil painting above it of a magnificent horse, almost life size, in a stiff, dressage pose. Katie studied its sleek chestnut haunches and cropped tail, marveling at the painter's skill.

The edge of the room was lined with large sofas with curved polished legs, but not much other furniture. She supposed she could be in a waiting room where guests gathered before heading through the double doors on the other side.

She padded quietly across the carpet to see if those doors led anywhere exciting, hoping that she wouldn't find them locked. The doors were tall and narrow, each one intricately paneled. She put her hand on one of the crystal doorknobs, and turned it. It creaked open and she looked inside.

She gasped with pleasure and surprise. It was a real ballroom with a beautiful parquet floor and chandeliers hanging from the ceiling. Along one wall hung tall windows, curved at the top, at regular intervals, each letting in a shaft of sunlight. On the other side—echoing the windows—were tall, gilt-framed mirrors as elegant as the windows. Drawn in by the sheer loveliness, she took a few tentative steps into the room before she noticed the ceiling. A domed, painted ceiling depicted the heavens, again with shafts of light coming down. She turned slowly and gazed in wonder.

The colors were vivid and spectacular—a bright blue sky with delicate white clouds where baby angels peeped down.

What a delight it must have been to dance here! This place put the railway hotel in the shade, for sure. Katie turned around and around, her feet spinning easily on the mellow golden floor. She allowed herself to imagine the music—a string quartet perhaps, playing something light and flirtatious. She could hear the sound of the guests' laughter, champagne glasses tinkling during toasts, and the rustle of silk taffeta. The men, handsome and witty, all looking out for a pretty girl who'd let them write their name on her dance card.

"Do you like to dance?"

"Yes," she breathed, though she had sworn she'd never like it again after Tom, and then her heart lurched and she opened her eyes.

*This was not an imagined conversation.*

His lordship was by the door. She had not heard him wheel in.

"So do I," he said, and in those three little words she heard such inexpressible sadness that she could feel his pain in her own heart.

What could she say? She faltered, feeling like a fool.

"Forgive me, sir, I opened the door and when I saw the ceiling I just had to have a look."

"It's my favorite room in the whole house."

He seemed almost human, Katie thought, not a bit like the unreasonable individual she'd met yesterday. She glanced up again at the extraordinary ceiling. "I've never seen anything like it. Beauty beyond compare."

When she looked back at him, he had a look in his eyes she couldn't read—a faint hint of amusement, perhaps?

Then an idea struck her. "Why don't you use it as your room, sir, then you could lie here and look up at that every day?"

As soon as the words escaped, she knew she was being much too forward. She shouldn't be talking to him like that, telling him what to do. He was not a man you could order around.

And yet, he didn't rebuke her. He was silent for a moment, and then he spoke. "Because I like to remember this room as it once was, before the war."

She nodded. She could understand that.

Katie could see that he would have been tall if he had been able to stand. His hair, cut into a classic short back and sides, was fair. The longer locks of hair that swept back from his forehead were definitely blond, while the shorter bits at the back were a deep honey color. His eyebrows were honey colored, too. His light blue eyes—his most striking feature—were bright and clear, but melancholy. His aristocratic face was pale when it wasn't pink with anger or embarrassment, and his mouth—she couldn't help but notice that his mouth was soft and sensual. It was a young man's mouth with lips a girl might like to kiss, if he was even slightly more approachable.

"I'll show you the rest of the house . . . well, the ground floor, at least," he said.

She hesitated, feeling awkward with him. She realized she had forgotten all about saying "good morning, my lord," like she'd practiced and it would be silly to say it now.

He wasn't going to take no for an answer. "Come along."

She was in no position to refuse. He was her employer.

He wheeled himself to the far end of the ballroom to another pair of double doors that opened to the rest of the house. She followed him obediently, her footsteps echoing as she went.

Together they looked into each of the quiet, lonely rooms. The billiard room adjoined the ballroom, where someone had abandoned the table in the middle of a game, as if they had intended to return in five minutes but their absence had turned into several years. The ladies' drawing room was swathed in dust covers. The Long Gallery displayed gloomy-looking oil paintings of Michael's ancestors. Then they turned another corner and went down a dark hallway that led back to the other side of the house. They peered into the conservatory that stood as an entryway of sorts to the formal garden beyond. It had once held masses of tropical plants, his lordship explained, but it was empty now. It would be wasteful to heat it in wartime.

"The kitchen and scullery you have seen already," he said, as they made their way back through to the entrance hall again on the grand circuit. "The only room you haven't been in, except for my own, is this one."

He asked her to open the dark paneled door for him, because the handle was mounted too high.

"The library," he said.

It was dark and sober, the walls were lined with books and there were low button-back chairs in dark leather scattered about. A globe stood in the center of the room, and Michael reached out and set it spinning as he passed by in one languid movement. It spun noiselessly on its well-oiled brass stand, gradually slowing down.

"You can read here, if you wish, Miss Rafferty."

"Thank you," she said, scanning the shelves, seeing a lot of dark red, leather-bound books. "That's very kind." She wondered why on earth he was being so friendly.

"I don't know that you'll find anything especially gripping. The books are mostly about agriculture and equine diseases, I'm afraid."

Equine means horses, she thought, mentally congratulating herself. "Why's that, sir?"

"Because horse-breeding was our livelihood before the war. We only started growing food when the Ministry of Agriculture told us we had to."

Katie wondered why he used the royal "we" but she just nodded politely and tried to look wise beyond her years.

"Perhaps you might find that a more fruitful source of entertainment." He inclined his head in the direction of an old gramophone player on the other side of the room—an impressive contraption with a big fluted trumpet to amplify the sound.

She smiled in delight and ran over to see which records he owned. They were housed in a polished wooden rack beside the gramophone, and she drew them out one by one to have a peek at the titles. He had quite a variety: sultry female singers and lively dance music, some jazz and some famous classical composers, even some American bands. She blew the dust off one of the records, and wondered how to ask permission to play it. She'd love to hear something lively, something fun.

"Put it back," he said gently, "I can't bear to hear music at the moment."

"Oh, I'm sorry," she said. "Only . . . this one isn't miserable at all."

"They all make me feel absolutely ghastly. You'll have to wait until I'm not around. Actually you'll have to wait until Jessop isn't around either. Then you can play them if you must. Don't let the children break them."

"Of course not, sir." She put the record back, glad she hadn't asked.

"You've seen the ground floor," he said, changing the subject. "The rest you can explore for yourself. Were you planning to go out, Miss Rafferty? Or do you feel the cold very acutely?"

She was still wearing her coat, and carrying her old woolen beret. She blushed. "I was just off to the village, sir, to post a letter to me mam. She'll want to hear that I'm settling in."

"Forgive me, for detaining you."

"It's no matter, sir. I enjoyed touring the house."

She turned to go, but he called her back.

"There is one more thing, Miss Rafferty."

"Yes, sir? What is it?"

He paused, as if this was difficult for him. "I do remember meeting you before."

She stiffened. So that was why he was being so nice to her—he wanted to soften her up so she would admit it all.

*No.* She refused to acknowledge that night.

He looked up at her. "You remember, too, don't you?"

Of course she hadn't forgotten his face. What woman on earth would forget the face of the man who had saved her life? But Katie wanted to forget. She needed to forget. "I've never seen you before in my life, sir, until I came here to look after the children," she lied, staunchly.

He let out a heavy sigh. "God knows I'm changed, Katie, but I'm the same man I was that day."

She was horrified to realize that he had used her first name. "I am sure you must be mistaken, sir. You must have danced with many girls and perhaps you once met an Irish girl like me."

"We didn't meet at a dance, and you know it!"

"It was someone else, sir." She recognized a note of rising hysteria in her voice as she tried to make him believe her fantasy.

He stared at her, frowning in surprise.

She backed away and dug in her pocket for her letter. "I really must go and post this, sir. I'm sorry!"

She took a deep breath and glanced toward the door. "I swear to you—it was someone else!"

His tone was cool and level. "Yes, I expect it was."

She turned and ran from the house, her feelings whirling about inside her. She wanted freedom, and fresh air, and to hurry along at top speed until her emotions subsided and she felt calmer again.

She went through the gate, which she remembered to clang shut behind her. She slowed down to a normal brisk walk, and set off in the direction of the village. She hoped it was not quite as far as the railway station. But even a moderately long walk would give her time to gather her composure.

His words rang in her head. "I do remember meeting you before," he had said, in that crisp, cultured voice of his when she had desperately hoped he wouldn't recognize her. At least he had seemed willing to play along when she refused to discuss it. She was grateful to him for that. She would put all her old troubles behind her, start anew, despite this connection to her past.

By the time she reached her destination, she felt much better.

Market Farrenden was charming. It boasted an old country pub, painted white with black beams and a thatched roof; a row of shops surrounding the village green; and a little stone church squatting in the middle, with a clock that said ten to three, even though it was only a quarter past eleven. Katie was thoroughly enchanted by it all.

All she had to do now was find the post office. It didn't seem to be one of the shops that faced onto the green.

A young policeman, in uniform and pushing a bicycle, stopped to help her.

"Are you lost, miss?"

"How did you know I was a stranger?" she said, in surprise.

"I know everyone who lives here. The Gerries could never plant a spy in Market Farrenden," he smiled. "I'd have them routed in the first half hour."

"I hope you don't think I'm a spy, Constable. I should hate to get myself arrested on my very first morning," she said, in a teasing tone.

The young constable's eyes twinkled, and a warning light came on inside Katie's heart. *No flirting. Ever again. Remember?*

"I know who you are," he said. "You're the little Irish girl that Mrs. Mallory got for his lordship."

"I'm here for the evacuees," Katie corrected. This young policeman had made it sound as if she were a hamper from Fortnum and Masons. He was quite a pleasant young man, though a little paunchy, and when he stopped to adjust his helmet, she could see he was going prematurely bald.

"Yes. Market Farrenden won't know what hit it, come tomorrow lunchtime. We haven't had any London ones, before. You never know what you're going to get with evacuees, do you? I hope there's no criminal element among them."

He walked with her, wheeling his bicycle, to the post office. Katie could tell from the way he kept smiling at her that she had made quite an impression, which was not her intention at all.

He almost wheeled his bike straight into the bright red pillar box outside the post office, and he blushed furiously when Katie touched his sleeve in warning.

"Here you are, Miss. Good luck tomorrow. I might see you there, at the village hall."

Katie thought that was entirely likely, given the length of time he spent shaking her hand. "Goodbye, Constable."

"Perkins, Arthur Perkins," he said. He got on his bicycle and wobbled away from the curb. She smiled as she watched him ride down the street. He'd boosted her confidence a little.

She felt for the letter in her pocket. Yes. It was there. She was a lucky girl; she had a new job, a new life, and a safe place to stay. Maybe 1941 would even be fun.

# Chapter Three

Friday morning Katie decided she would wear the pearls. She was supposed to pick up the children at the village hall at half-past eleven. She waited nervously in the grand entrance for the car to arrive, wishing she didn't have to go alone. At least she didn't have to walk this time.

An old black Austin, square and dependable like a large upright biscuit tin, pulled up alongside the front steps. The driver introduced himself as Harold Hammond, who lodged at Home Farm and worked on the estate. Katie hopped in, and Harold started whistling as they drove along the country lanes toward the village. He kept looking across at Katie's legs, though she had tried to arrange the A-line skirt of her winter suit as modestly as possible.

"When's your afternoon off, then?" he said.

"I don't think I have an afternoon off," Katie said. It certainly hadn't been mentioned during the embarrassing discussion with his lordship the day she arrived.

"All the girls at the house gets an afternoon off." He gave her a bit of a wink. "Don't be shy."

"Well, I'm sorry, but I don't know when mine is, Mr. Hammond."

"Harry," he said. "Harold was me father's name."

She smiled, weakly.

"Been to the Dog and Whistle yet, have you?" he persisted.

"Is that a public house?"

"Best in the village," he said, patting her knee.

Katie glanced down at his hand as if a haddock with its guts hanging out had just landed on her lap. Hammond moved his hand a little further up her thigh, ruching up her skirt a bit. Katie would have protested, but she noticed a horse and cart looming on the road ahead. She nearly let out a scream. Harry moved smartly and got his hands back on the wheel. He veered sharply and missed the cart, but the horse looked a bit nervous as they passed. The man driving the cart shouted an epithet and waved his fist, but Harry wasn't flustered.

"Yes. You'll like the old Dog and Whistle," he said. "All the little maids from the house like it there. Nice little garden round the back, too."

Katie was annoyed. "Mrs. Jessop said it was only five minutes to the village by car."

"Five or ten," he said, with a smirk. "Depends on which road you take. Lovers' Lane might take half an hour."

"We must take the shortest route possible, Mr. Hammond. I promised I'd be there at eleven. Now please don't be delaying me any longer!"

"I bet it's Wednesday," he said, smiling to himself. "Your afternoon off."

\*

Mrs. Mallory was manning the village hall, the temporary home of forty-seven evacuees from Stepney in the East End of London. This was seven more than she had been expecting, which was causing her a bit of grief. Finding several more families who, at a moment's notice, would agree to take in a grubby little Londoner or two was no mean feat. Meanwhile people were arriving to take the children home, and sometimes the children and the adults made a fuss about their match. The curate's wife was trying to help, but at twenty-three years old, she had no experience with children, except for the slight bulge caused by her five-month pregnancy.

"Marjory! Marjory! What would you do about this?" she kept calling.

Mrs. Mallory was trying to make sure that each child remembered to take his coat, gas mask, and ration book. One of the boys had raided the Women's Institute store cupboards and found a huge pair of old dressmaking scissors. He was bobbing about dangerously with them when Mrs. Mallory noticed the shenanigans.

"For heaven's sake, Gladys, you can't let him run around with those! Take them away from him immediately."

"I'm so sorry, Marjory, but I've been dealing with an absolute crisis in the lavatory. It's totally blocked, and there's a long queue forming. One of the little tykes has wet himself already."

Mrs. Mallory rose, and took a deep breath. In one swift movement, she snatched the scissors away from George and sailed down to the back of the hall to investigate the water closet. Gladys hurried after her.

They gazed into the depths of the lavatory pan trying to work out what had gone wrong.

"It's funny—it looks sort of furry, doesn't it? You don't think a rat could have gotten in there do you?"

"I can't think why it should want to," Mrs. Mallory replied crisply as she briefly disappeared to hunt up a plunger. The two both took a go at the pan, and Mrs. Mallory was exceptionally energetic, but to no avail. It remained resolutely blocked.

"Well, all the little boys will have to go around the back of the building and relieve themselves by the hedge," she ordered, while Gladys went pale. "Girls! Form a line, and follow Gladys to the vicarage next door. No dawdling. Gladys, give me that plunger, there's a dear!"

*

Katie arrived at the village hall feeling flustered. Harry Hammond had definitely taken the circuitous route, and Mrs. Mallory appeared on the steps, brandishing the plunger in one hand. She looked very disapproving when she saw who had given Katie a lift into the village. Harry obviously had a reputation.

"I hope you gave Hammond no encouragement?"

"None whatsoever, ma'am," Katie replied. Katie had no intention of making the same mistakes again. The car drive with Hammond only served to remind her how predatory men could be.

Mrs. Mallory tossed aside the plunger and took Katie to meet her four boys. Mrs. Mallory had chosen some of the bigger ones because of all that lovely open space at Farrenden Manor. She didn't want to inflict the very young ones on Lord Farrenden, she said. At least Katie would be spared the whole drama of littlies who wet the bed.

The oldest one, Roy, was a dirty young tough who would probably grow up into a big, bull-headed young man someday. At the moment, he was quite a bit shorter than Katie, with a chubby face and a mop of dark curly hair. She guessed he was twelve or thirteen.

"I want me own bed," he announced, folding his arms across his chest.

Katie was used to people with London accents, since she had lived there for months, but she was a little unsettled by Roy's manner, which was discontented and aggressive.

"Possibly headed for a life of crime," Mrs. Mallory whispered, when she handed over the first of the precious ration books. "But his mother died not long ago in the bombing, so I suppose we must reserve our judgment."

The next one was called Alfie, and he looked like a little elf. He had a pointed chin and fronds of mousy hair hanging in a tuft over his forehead. He was sitting on an old kitchen chair reading a pamphlet about how to operate the fire extinguisher.

The next two were brothers, Bob and George.

"We're twins," they announced.

"So you are, so you are!" said Katie, and then blushed because she knew she sounded like a right little colleen, fresh off the boat. She knelt down to have a closer look at these two. They were exactly the same height, and very, very similar, but perhaps not identical, Katie decided.

Katie smiled at each of them, and did up a button on George's coat for him. His label said "George Kilby, Pleasant Gardens,

Stepney." Katie smiled. She'd been to Stepney once last year, and she hadn't noticed many pleasant gardens. Not compared with the glorious green landscapes of County Clare at least.

"Where's your label, little man?" Katie asked the other boy. "Did you lose it on the train?"

Bob looked a bit worried, as if he'd been accused of doing something wrong.

"It's no matter," Katie said, "we've got your brother here to tell us who you are."

Bob rewarded her with a shy smile.

"They look like fine boys, Mrs. Mallory," Katie said, mainly for the benefit of the children. It must be very hard on them to leave their own homes and their parents and everything they knew.

Katie checked the ration books, counted the gas masks, and herded them toward the door. Hammond had parked at the foot of the steps, and he was leaning against the car, enjoying a cigarette in the afternoon sun.

"You'll have no problem at all with this lot," Mrs. Mallory said brightly.

Katie got the feeling she'd been saying that rather frequently this morning. She went down the steps with her band of little brothers, glad that she wasn't going to be alone with Hammond on the journey back to Farrenden Manor.

*

Michael heard the noise in the hall. They sounded like extremely excitable young people, with their rough London accents and their noisy boots. He heard strident little voices talking about ack-ack guns and dog fights. Katie must have told them he used to be a pilot—little Irish chatterbox that she was, she wouldn't be able to keep anything to herself. Not like English girls. He sighed. The end of peace and tranquility.

He sighed again, deeply, when he heard them pretending to be Spitfires. People were in love with bloody Spitfires, he thought bitterly. Michael's flying career was over when the Spitfires came on the scene. He had flown a Hurricane, and he missed her like a favorite horse. She was a wonderful plane, and he could make her do anything he wanted. With his own bare hands, he had filed the heads off the rivets all along her fuselage just to make her go a little bit faster—and she thundered through the sky like a shooting star. He used to feel on top of the world when he was inside the cockpit. He supposed she was smashed to smithereens in somebody's cornfield now.

He knew what would happen if he went out there to introduce himself. The youngsters would be curious about the wheelchair. They'd want to know all the details of the accident. Children weren't the least bit shy about that sort of thing. They had to be taught not to ask.

He could hear them asking questions now. Is the house haunted, they wanted to know. God knows how many times Michael had fielded that question. Every second visitor longed to find a headless knight in the butler's pantry or a blood-stained wench in the upstairs loo. Sometimes he thought he ought to make one up just to make himself popular with guests, but these days he was far too jaded to try.

Suddenly he heard an almighty crash. Michael immediately knew what it was. The bloody little hooligans had knocked over Charlie, the suit of armor that stood in the corner of the hall by the umbrella stand. His face twitched with annoyance. It was not the first time Charlie had fallen over by any means, but it was the sheer timing of the incident. Those wretched children had been in his house only four minutes and they were already destroying the place. He could hear hysterical shrieks of laughter after the initial shock of felling Charlie had worn off. Where was Katie, and why didn't she keep them under control?

*

"Is he damaged?" Katie said in alarm, gazing down at what looked like a metal corpse lying on the hall floor.

"Don't think so, Miss. He's meant to take the knocks, isn't he? Looks tough as old boots to me." Roy gave the helpless suit of armor a sharp kick, and the sound of reverberating metal echoed around the entrance hall.

Katie heard an angry bark of displeasure behind her, and nearly leaped out of her skin.

"Why are you all making so much noise? I'm trying to work. I have letters from the Ministry of Agriculture that require my immediate attention!"

Katie turned sharply. It was amazing how his lordship's well-oiled wheels enabled him to creep up on people.

"My humble apologies, sir. We had a bit of an accident. We're trying to sort it out now."

"Looked more like you were putting the boot in, to me," Michael said, turning on Roy. "Why don't you pick on someone who can put up a bit of fight? Not much of a challenge with Charlie, is there? Well, boy, speak up! What kind of a coward are you?"

Great, thought Katie. He's got off on the wrong foot with Roy already, and we've only just come through the door.

Roy folded his arms over his chest in a provocative manner. "I ain't no coward, Mister, and I've got a good right hook, make no mistake. What did you call him? Charlie? You ought to put him out for the old iron man, in my opinion."

"Which nobody asked for, did they?" Michael interjected, sharply. "Kindly remember that you are a guest in my house, and I'll thank you not to be so rude about my parents' treasured possessions."

"Yes, for goodness sake, Roy, this is his lordship you're talking to!" Katie reminded him.

"He should be melted down and made into something useful, like a machine gun," said Roy.

"Who should be melted down? Do you mean him?" The smallest boy, Bob, was pointing his finger at Michael.

There was a horrified pause, while everyone pondered this last remark. Alfie obviously wanted to laugh, Katie was sure of it, but he managed to contain himself. Michael's icy blue eyes stared at Bob, and Katie hoped desperately that he didn't turn on the little boy and shout him down. It was an innocent misunderstanding from a child.

Then Michael gave a snort of laughter. "Well, perhaps I will see active duty again if I manage to get myself melted down and made into a machine gun!"

Even Roy seemed to think that was funny.

Katie gave a tiny sigh of relief. She realized they hadn't stopped for the pleasantries yet. "This is Roy Luckens, from Stepney, your lordship. And over here we have Alfie Nicholls, and twins, Bob and George Kilby."

Michael stuck out his hand to shake Alfie's, the child standing nearest to him. "Delighted to make your acquaintance, young man. I'm Michael Melt-me-Down Farrenden, peer of the realm."

"What's a peer of the elm?" George asked.

"It's a toff, that's what it is," said Roy.

"Yes it is," Michael agreed and extended his hand in Roy's direction. After a moment's surly hesitation, Roy unfolded his arms long enough to shake Michael's hand. Katie waited patiently while Michael finished the routine with all of them.

"Now children," she said, when the handshaking ritual was over. "This is a valuable suit of armor. If we break him we will all have to contribute our pocket money for about the next fifteen years to mend him. So this must never happen again. Roy, Alfie, you get over on the other side and I'll help you lift him up."

They hauled Charlie into a standing position again, and Katie adjusted his visor, with unnecessary care.

"How's that, sir?" she murmured.

Michael could sense her embarrassment. He gave a short sigh. "He always did look a little drunk and disorderly, I suppose."

The children lost interest and started circling the hall, pretending to be Spitfires again, gunning each other from time to time with great enthusiasm. The roaring noise they made as the four of them pretended to take off was indeed almost as deafening as a real RAF scramble.

"For heaven's sake, Miss Rafferty! What's the matter with them?"

"Nothing, sir, they are perfectly normal healthy children. They need to work off their energy, that's all. They've been cooped up on a train and trying to sit still in the village hall all morning."

Michael looked at them in dismay. The two younger ones were circling the room with their arms outstretched, the older boys were standing on the tapestry chairs gunning at each other with much gusto and wild staccato sound effects. "When do they get tired? What time can you put them to bed?"

"About eight o'clock, I suppose. They're not babies."

"Eight o'clock!" he glanced at his wristwatch. "That's not for another seven hours!"

"I know. I'll feed them lunch in a minute. Then I'll take them outside for a run round the estate. I thought they might enjoy a walk by the river, as long as none of them fall in and drown."

"Oh, drown as many of them as you like. I don't mind."

"Sir, that's an awful thing to say. Their parents have entrusted them to us, and I am sure they are each very precious to them."

"Sorry."

"I thought I'd give them their tea at five o'clock in the kitchen, followed by some as-yet-unscheduled activities, and eventually it will be bath time. After that I'll read stories to the little ones and put them to bed."

"Good God," said Michael, and turned his pale blue eyes upon her, "how grueling! However long do we have to put up with them?"

Katie shrugged. "Until the end of the war."

Michael rolled his eyes in horror.

\*

At bedtime, Katie dealt with the inevitable fight about who would get the best bed. The one by the window was deemed "preferred," and Alfie expressed an immediate interest in it. The twins thought it looked big enough for them to share, even though there were enough beds for everybody to have one each, and Roy thought that he should have first dibs, being the oldest, the biggest, and the toughest.

Roy won, of course, no contest.

Alfie looked very put out. Katie couldn't help feeling a little sorry for him. "Don't worry, little man, you won't be up here much during the day. Not with the whole estate to explore—and look! This bed has a nice little bedside lamp."

That seemed to mollify him, and Katie soon realized why. His suitcase, which was very small but weighed a ton, was almost entirely filled with books and magazines. He had only one other change of clothes, a very ragged pair of pajamas, and a moth-eaten teddy bear with one eye. Katie had a feeling he'd packed the case himself.

Katie concentrated on getting the little ones unpacked, sorting through their clothes to see if their mothers had packed everything they needed. Katie couldn't understand why Bob didn't have a suitcase. George had a case with all his clothes carefully marked G. Kilby. Surely Mrs. Kilby must have packed a similar suitcase for his brother, with clothes carefully labeled B. Kilby?

"Did you leave your suitcase on the train, Bob?"

"Dunno. Maybe."

"But you did set out from London with one?"

"Not sure."

"How can you not remember something like that?"

"Dunno. I can always wear George's clothes, Miss. He won't

mind and we are the same size."

"I suppose you'll have to, for tomorrow at least. Though George doesn't have that many clothes to lend you."

Bob's haircut was another mystery. It was awful. George had a conventional short back and sides like a little mini-adult. Bob's hair looked like it had been chewed off with nail scissors. It was choppy and clumpy round the back. Katie began to wonder if favoritism existed in the twins' family. Some parents singled out one child for special privileges, although she thought it was more unusual in the case of twins.

"I don't know what we'll send you to school in, come Monday. I'll have to talk to his lordship about it. He might possibly agree to pay for a school uniform; I hope we can get something before clothing goes on ration."

"There's always the black market," Roy said, sitting on the edge of his bed, trying out the springs.

Katie looked up sharply. She hadn't expected a twelve-year-old to be quite so worldly wise.

"My mum had a couple of contacts, if you're prepared to keep quiet about it," Roy continued. "But it will cost you."

"Thank you, Roy. I'm sure you are trying to be helpful, but I think we'll stick to abiding by the law if we can," said Katie, going over to the window to check that the blackout curtains were properly in place. "Speaking of which. I have a list of some basic dos and don'ts that his lordship wrote up for us. I think we'd all better have a good look at it. Especially as things didn't go so well when we first arrived. You must be very careful of that suit of armor, for a start."

"Charlie!" Roy snorted, despairingly.

"What did the old geezer call himself—Michael Melted Down Farringtale?"

"Farrenden," Katie corrected. "Like Farrenden Market."

"Fancy having a whole village named after you."

Alfie chipped in. "More than one, Roy. There was a Great Farrenden and a Little Farrenden and a Farrenden Saint Mary—I saw them on a map."

"Proper toff he is and no mistake," Roy observed. "Never met one in a wheelchair before."

"Toff on wheels."

"Sounds like a good name for a comic strip," said Alfie. "You any good at drawing?"

"Nah. I'm useless," Roy said, groveling about in his rucksack. "Football. That's what I'm good at."

Roy pulled out a shabby, battered old soccer ball, with not quite sufficient air inside it, and before Katie could stop him he kicked it with great force at the wall and shouted "Yes! Goal! He's scored again for Tottenham!"

"Not in here, you don't, young man." Katie hurled herself forward and grabbed the ball before it rolled under one of the beds. "I'm confiscating this until tomorrow."

"That's mine, Miss. Give it back!"

Katie held it aloft, with the practiced skill of a person with a lot of younger brothers and sisters. "Tomorrow, Roy. Now get into that bed and start sleeping. Then tomorrow will come quick as a flash."

"I ain't sleepy, Miss."

"I don't imagine that you are, Roy, but it's been a long day and I think you should all do some pretend sleeping until the morning. You never know. Real sleep might just creep up on you."

It's creeping up on me, she thought. She was dog tired. Even the concrete bed seemed like an inviting prospect just now. "Last one into bed is a rotten egg!" she called, and watched them scramble in.

"It's Alfie. He's a rotten egg!" Roy said, in triumph, and Alfie rolled his eyes.

Then Bob's voice came from over in the corner. "There ain't no ghost, not really, is there, miss?"

"No. I never allow any ghosts to get past me," Katie promised. She turned out the light, and closed the door. She sent up a quick prayer to the saints. She'd need to become one to deal with this lot.

# Chapter Four

To Katie's surprise, Michael joined them at breakfast. Mrs. Jessop rolled his chair to the head of the table—looking very much as if she was acting against her better judgment—and Katie rushed around setting a place for him, wondering what on earth a huffy English lord would like for breakfast.

He buttered a piece of toast, very precisely, and said nothing. He pretended to read his newspaper while he ate. He was dressed, immaculately as ever, in a suit of clothes in Prince of Wales check. Inside the open collar of his shirt, he wore a silk cravat, knotted rather loosely, revealing the masculine lines of his neck. He cleared his throat and frowned at his newspaper as if something on the front page had offended him.

Katie told herself not to stare. She tried to concentrate on helping Bob and George with their boiled eggs and cutting up their bread into soldiers for them until she realized Michael was studying *her*.

Roy noticed too, and chirped up. "She looks like Rita Hayworth, don't she?"

Michael looked at him sharply and opened his mouth, but he seemed a little lost for words.

"Don't you think so, Mister?" said Roy. "Dead ringer for her if you ask me."

Katie could have died of embarrassment. Rita Hayworth, indeed!

A pink tinge of color rose in Michael's cheeks.

Alfie stepped in. "Maybe Mister Lord doesn't know a lot about films."

"He knows about Rita Hayworth," Roy insisted. "He's got a picture of her inside the lid of his shaving kit."

Michael dropped his piece of toast, and mortified horror

44

crossed his face. Alfie and the twins had a bit of a giggle, but the look on Michael's face silenced them.

Katie didn't know what to say, but she knew she had to salvage the situation, and fast.

She turned on Roy. "It's very rude to touch other people's things!" She turned to Michael and tried to placate him. "I'm so sorry sir, I didn't realize. I had no idea he'd gone into your washroom—"

"What the blazes were you doing with my shaving kit?" Michael said, cutting her off, leaning forward to speak to Roy.

Katie noticed that he didn't deny ownership of the picture.

"I thought I needed a shave," Roy announced, importantly.

"You needed a shave!" Michael exploded. "That's absurd when your chin is as smooth as a baby's bottom."

Roy scowled. He did have the face of a surly cherub, without a whisker in sight. "I'm shaving twice a week, and that's a fact," he insisted.

"I may have to write to your Auntie Madge, Roy," Katie began, knowing that tact was required with twelve-year-old boys, "to send you up a razor."

Michael snorted, but Katie sent a pleading look in his direction.

"Sir, he probably *will* be needing one before long, wouldn't you say?"

Michael glanced at Roy, and paused. Then he looked at Katie, and frowned.

Katie hoped she hadn't overstepped the mark. It was so important that everything go smoothly this morning. If his lordship went into one of his sarcastic tirades, if Roy behaved like a little East End tough, if it scared the other children on their first day . . . who knew where it would lead?

"Well, possibly," Michael conceded at last. "A blunt one, perhaps."

Katie didn't like the postscript, but Roy looked triumphant. He stuck his soft, chubby chin out in front of him, wiped his nose with the back of his hand, and took a big, provocative bite out of his toast and marmalade.

Katie rewarded him with a wide smile of relief.

"See!" Roy said. "She *does* look like Rita Hayworth, when she smiles."

Michael looked up and studied Katie's face as if she was an exhibit in the British Museum. "I suppose she does."

Then he returned to his newspaper and did not utter another word.

*

After breakfast, the children clattered into the hall to get their school satchels and Katie followed them, taking the opportunity on the way to explain to his lordship the problem with Bob's missing suitcase.

"I don't know if there's any point in hoping that it will turn up," she said.

"Probably not. It may have been stolen—people will do anything for clothing now that the shortages are starting to bite."

"I wish they'd start proper rationing for clothing, to be honest, like they do with food. At least it would be fair. I was wondering if you had any old clothes of your own that you don't use any more. I might be able to cut them down to make a pair of school shorts for Bob. My sewing isn't up to a blazer, but I might manage a pair of pants."

"There's a stack of my old clothes upstairs in the Chinese Room. It used to be my room when I was . . . " he obviously didn't want to say something like *able-bodied*. "It was my room when I was at school. Take anything you want. There's even an old dinner jacket in there somewhere that you can cut that up if you like."

Katie was surprised. "That's very generous of you, sir. But are you sure you won't be needing it?"

He scowled. "Oddly enough, I haven't felt the need to dress up much, stuck in this thing."

Katie nearly commented that his lordship always looked "dressed up." He seemed to have an endless array of elegant, stylishly tailored garments, and though none of them were new, it was all of the very best quality. He could have posed for society magazines. In fact, Katie realized with a slight shock, he probably had.

She turned to leave, but Michael called her back.

"There won't be a repeat performance of yesterday's bad behavior, will there? The children cannot be allowed to racket about in my house like bandits." He waved his hand imperiously at the chairs on either side of the door that led to his rooms. "My mother spent hours making those needlepoint covers for the hall chairs, don't you know?"

"No, I hadn't realized. Maybe we could put those chairs in a safer place, sir, where they won't come to any harm?"

"Perhaps the little ruffians could be taught to treat other people's things with more respect. My parents would have a fit if they could see what's going on in their house."

For the first time, Katie wondered what had happened to Michael's parents, but it didn't seem the right moment to ask.

"I'll do my level best, sir, to encourage the children to be more orderly and civilized."

"Thank you."

She thanked him again for his generosity with the clothing, and went to find her hat and coat. She had promised to walk down to the village with the children to show them where the school was, ready for Monday morning.

She hoped, desperately, that the children would behave themselves on their first day. She had a feeling that for Roy, at least, that might be a bit of a challenge.

# Chapter Five

It was almost two weeks before Michael began to suspect what had happened. To understand the real reason Katie had walked back into his life. He sat in the bay window of his study watching her run around on the front lawn with the children. Her auburn hair kept escaping from her beret, curls bouncing as she moved. And he loved the way her slim skirt delineated her trim little figure. What a firecracker.

He picked up the receiver of the large black telephone that sat on his rosewood desk, and asked to speak to Mrs. Mallory.

"How did you manage to find her?" he wanted to know.

"Find who?"

Michael exhaled sharply. "Katie Rafferty, the Irish girl."

"She was recommended to me by a friend of a friend."

"Rubbish. She's the girl I met in London. The one I told you about," Michael insisted.

"Are you sure? There's a coincidence!" Mrs. Mallory's deep plummy voice didn't lend itself well to feigning surprise.

"Don't give me that nonsense, Marjory. I told you I'd helped a girl out in a bombing raid, and the next thing I know she turns up on my bloody doorstep."

Mrs. Mallory must have realized she was caught out, so she gave in gracefully. "You did say you wished you knew what had happened to her, dear."

"I didn't say I wanted her living under my roof!"

"Do you have some complaint about the girl? Has she disappointed you in some way?"

"Not yet."

"Then you must give her a chance. You helped her before. She needs your help now, she needs somewhere to live."

"How did you trace her? I didn't tell you her name—I didn't know it myself."

"Michael, dear, you told me the girl was in labor when the station was bombed. It was obvious that there must have been dozens of witnesses, and it didn't take long to find somebody who knew where she was. You could have found her yourself if you'd put a little effort into it."

"Very ingenious. Why go to all that trouble to find someone I only mentioned once, in passing?"

"You mentioned her several times, Michael, when you were recovering from your accident. Each time I came to see you in hospital. You seemed very troubled about it."

Mrs. Mallory could be right. He had been in so much pain and distress after the accident, on so much morphine, that he might have said just about anything about anybody. He hoped he hadn't made a complete fool of himself.

"I wondered what happened to her, that's all."

"Yes. And now you have the chance to find out. Aren't you going to thank me?"

"No, Marjory. This is hideously embarrassing for the girl and for me. She denies all knowledge of that night in London, you know?"

"Does she, dear? Well, you must try using your charm. It hasn't failed you yet, has it?"

Michael closed his eyes in frustration. Charm, indeed. As if he had any charm now. A broken man who couldn't do anything, that's all he was. "You should not have interfered, Marjory."

"You need a bit of a shake-up. And Katie's a little spitfire, so I'm told."

"Will everyone stop going on about bloody Spitfires!"

"Temper, temper!"

Michael sighed. Mrs. Mallory only meant to be kind. "Do you know what happened to her baby?" he said.

Mrs. Mallory paused. "There was some hearsay, but it wouldn't be fair to Katie to pass it on. She'll tell you herself, when she's ready."

Mrs. Mallory refused to divulge anything else, so Michael put down the phone and gazed out of the window at Katie, so he could continue his surveillance of her.

He always tried to be discreet and surreptitious, but he had taken up watching Katie whenever he got the chance. He didn't mean to be sneaky, but it was dreadfully boring being housebound, and she intrigued him. If he knew she was in the kitchen, he would wheel himself silently along the corridor and stay in the shadows to peek through the doorway, hoping she wouldn't notice him there.

He had watched her cleaning and scrubbing the floor. He'd seen her check her lipstick in the reflection of a copper pot hanging on the wall. He'd seen her sorting out his old clothes on the kitchen table, assembling a set of things that Bob could wear. In the late afternoons, when the children came back from school, he wheeled his chair through to the back of the house, and watched them through the window. He saw the children running and laughing outside in the paddock—and Katie teaching them how to play leapfrog and some Irish version of tag. She obviously adored children, so why was she not looking after her own?

Michael heard all about the first day crisis with Roy—how he picked a fight and achieved a sort of celebrity status on the playground as a result. Katie gave him a good talking to, then promised him a brand new set of knuckle jacks if he got through the rest of the week without incident.

She was a determined young woman for sure, and she knew how to manage the little blighters. She took them all down to the village shop to buy new sets of knuckle jacks. She taught the little ones how to play. She removed a knuckle jack that George had experimentally inserted, with tearful consequences, up his own nose. She organized a system of gold stars and peppermint drops for homework done, with extra credit for a low inkblot count. She held races to see who could shine his shoes for school the fastest, and she made bedtime into a great game.

Michael sighed. He wouldn't have minded playing a few bedtime games with her himself—if things had only been different.

\*

Katie stood in the kitchen with her hands on her hips, confronting Mrs. Jessop about the food. "You're telling me that there isn't even butter for the children's tea? Here, on a farm!"

"No, and the margarine is almost gone, too."

"Where did it go?"

Mrs. Jessop was silent.

"And what am I supposed to give the children for their tea? Bread and water?" Katie's hackles rose and she knew she was on dangerous ground.

"It wouldn't hurt them, just for once."

"But it's absurd! We've got the coupons for something a bit more substantial than that—I'll go down to the village and pick up some supplies if you'll find the ration books."

"The coupons are all gone, Miss Rafferty. There's a war on, you know."

Every time someone uttered that sentence, Katie wanted to scream.

"Mrs. Jessop. The children have precious little in their sandwiches each day, and we've had bread and jam for supper all week. On Saturday, we had mushrooms on toast, and the long-awaited Sunday lunch was an egg flan with only the merest hint of cheese in it. What, exactly, has happened to our meat ration?"

"It's been very difficult to get meat this week."

"Then let me go down to the butcher's and see what I can find today. Where are the ration books?"

"I told you. We haven't got the coupons."

"We seem to be going in circles in this discussion. You've been given four extra ration books only last Friday; five if you include mine that you made me hand over when I arrived. I know exactly how many coupons were in mine, and the children's books were almost full. We have plenty of coupons for what we need today, unless you've already spent them."

"Are you suggesting that I would misappropriate the children's food?"

"It is looking more and more as if you have, since you won't show me the ration books."

"Well! I won't stand for this." Mrs. Jessop grabbed her coat and hat. "Over thirty years I've cooked for the family, and never had any complaints until you come along. You can cook supper yourself and see how well you can manage it, then, Miss Upstart Rafferty, because I won't stay here and be insulted."

"You'll have to leave me the ration books, because there isn't anything to cook."

But Mrs. Jessop was already putting on her coat.

"I'll have to tell his lordship," Katie threatened.

"His lordship doesn't trouble himself with domestic matters, Miss Rafferty. He's always had complete faith in me."

It was true, Katie knew. Michael's disinterest in the way that the house was run was legendary. But she wasn't backing down now. "The ration books?" she demanded.

"You'll lose your job over this," Mrs. Jessop almost spat the words at Katie. "I'll give notice tomorrow, and I'll only come back when you're gone, you little Irish hussy!" With that, she stormed out through the kitchen door, slamming it in bitter protest.

"And good riddance!" Katie yelled, still raging inside, though what her employer would say when he found out what she'd done she dreaded to think. She sighed and shook her head, only to turn around and see him in the doorway.

She gasped. He ought to wear a bell, she thought, so he couldn't slink up behind her like a cat. She knew he had probably heard the whole thing, but he gave her a questioning stare.

"What the blazes were you saying to Jessop?"

"I asked her to give me back the children's ration books."

"You said a hell of a lot more than that, Katie. She's gone home. She's talking about giving me her notice."

"Good. You'll be better off without her."

"You can't take it upon yourself to dismiss my servants!"

"You can't see what's going on in front of your eyes, can you? Not even if you sit down to a pauper's meal every night!"

Michael's blue eyes flashed with anger and confusion.

Katie sighed. "She's stealing the coupons, sir. The meals she serves us aren't fit for the pigs. The children need the little bit of meat that we can get for them—they're growing kids. If you ask me, she's stealing our rations to feed that great idle lump she calls a husband. He gets a nice beef dinner, and we get the leavings."

Michael frowned. It was perfectly clear. He sighed.

"For God's sake, Katie. You should have approached me if you had a complaint."

"And what, may I ask, would you have done? Precisely nothing. I can't have the kiddies going hungry, sir. They fight all the time. They hit each other. They steal from other children at school, and they might even get rickets or something terrible like that. Jessop has no right to their food!"

"No." He paused, taking it all in. "But she was my last servant from the old days," he said pitifully. "She knows how the place ticks, Katie. She wasn't the best, but now we have nothing. We have six people to feed, and no cook."

"I can cook, sir. It's getting hold of the food that I'm worried about. She still has the ration books." Katie looked out of the window, still rankling with anger. "And she wouldn't give them back, no matter how hard I tried."

Michael frowned. "Would it implicate her, if they were returned?" His tone of voice was softer, milder now.

Katie nodded. "She's spent the coupons."

"What do we do?"

"You could report her to the police," Katie suggested, but she knew the idea was a non-starter the minute it was out of her mouth.

Michael was horrified. "I couldn't do that to old Jessop after thirty years. We need to be more *diplomatic*, Katie."

"Yes, well, you sit at your desk being diplomatic and I'll steal something for our dinner."

*

Katie flounced across the kitchen, cheeks burning and auburn hair flying. She hunted around in the pantry and found flour and salt. She might be able to make soda bread. But the children needed a bit more than that after walking all the way home from the village school. On impulse, she grabbed her coat and rushed down the lane, heading for Home Farm. Maybe she could beg something to cook for dinner, just for tonight. She'd have to think of an excuse, though. Mrs. Jessop was taken ill, and the groceries hadn't been delivered. Something *diplomatic*.

What if she had burned her boots with his lordship? What if he gave her the sack? She hurtled down the lane, blinded by the tears that came unexpectedly into her eyes.

She almost ran smack into someone in her haste. It was Harry Hammond.

"Hullo! Where are you going in such a hurry, love?"

"Not now, Harry."

"You remember me name, then?" he said with a smug smile. He was chewing on a piece of straw, like a farmer in a comic book. "Old Mrs. Jessop was in a bit of a tizzy as well," he observed, philosophically. "Went past just half an hour ago."

"Jessop is a thief," Katie said, diplomacy be damned.

Hammond laughed. "You are a little cat among the pigeons, aren't you, my pretty little thing?"

"I'm not exactly 'little,' I will never be yours, and I object to being called a 'thing.' Get out of my way, Mr. Hammond. I have to get to Home Farm right away."

She stalked past him, misjudged her step, and fell. The cart had made ruts in the lane and they were full of water. She fell straight back into the puddle, much to her ignominy and embarrassment.

Hammond came over, laughing wildly, and offered her a hand. She took it, most reluctantly, and when she was nearly up he let her fall back and laughed some more. The second time she managed to get to her feet. She practically screamed at him to get out of her way, but he leaned forward and snatched the chance to kiss her on the cheek. She pushed him away and tried to stalk off.

"Katie, I know you're in a hurry to get to the farm," Hammond said, with a rather smug sort of laugh, "but have you taken into account the fact that I'm the one in charge there? If it's farm business your calling about, I'm the man you're needing to see."

Katie could have hit him, but he was right.

*

Dinner was on the hob and Katie was about ready to dish up. The boys had just been warned to clear their homework off the scrubbed pine table.

Michael appeared in the doorway and hesitated. Katie glanced questioningly at him. He didn't come into the room and didn't seem to want to go away.

"It smells good, Katie," he said, in a rather subdued tone of voice.

"It's a beef stew with a dash of Guinness in it. Maggie at Home Farm gave me the beef—with Hammond's permission of course—and George found some root vegetables in the back of the larder. There's soda bread to go with it, and apple pudding after. I was planning to feed the children straight away," she explained. "I will bring you some on a tray, sir, at your usual dinner time."

Michael gave an unexpected smile. "Katie, you don't expect me to come in to that marvelous aroma and then toddle off and wait for the leftovers, do you? That would be cruel."

"Of course we would be honored to have you eat with us, sir," she said. "I didn't like to presume."

"That's funny, you were quite presumptuous earlier," he observed.

"Yes, sir, I was. A bad case of hunger and a sense of injustice can do that."

"I see. I had a starving Irish rebel on my hands."

Katie felt herself giving way to a smile, though she hadn't quite forgiven him yet.

Alfie staggered to the table with a stack of plates, and the twins made a desultory attempt to set the table. Roy grabbed a knife and fork and started drumming with them, which made Michael frown with disapproval.

"Roy, we've no need for the percussion solo," Katie said. "Let's get some food into us, before we have another rebellion on our hands." She brought the fragrant, steaming dish to the table, and went back for the bread.

Michael took his place at the head of the table, rolling his chair into position and putting on the hand brakes. Bob found Michael a knife and fork, and smiled shyly at him. Bob had taken a real shine to "Mister Lord."

The soda bread had risen to perfection, and it smelled wonderful. Katie broke it into pieces and handed it around. "Eat up!" she encouraged, since the children were a little in awe of Michael.

Michael ate like a soldier who hadn't seen food for a week. "It's good, Katie, really good," he muttered between mouthfuls.

"Thank you," she said. She knew she was a good cook, but it was gratifying to hear him say it. Reassuring, too, after the whole fiasco this afternoon. She'd been in tears at Home Farm, thinking she was about to be sacked. Back in Ireland, her mam always said, "You're a good girl, Katie, but your besetting sin is losing your temper." Katie had cursed herself for her stupidity in talking back to his lordship, even though his lordship had definitely deserved it. Maggie, the farmer's wife, had made her a cup of tea and assured Katie it would all blow over.

"Do you still want me to pack my bags, sir?" Katie asked meekly. "Since I upset you so much when I spoke out of turn?"

The children set up a chorus of "No! No! You can't go!"

"No need to do anything rash, Katie," said Michael, and he glanced in the direction of the tureen in the center of the table to see if there were any second helpings.

Katie could see what he wanted and ladled more out for him. She saw him hesitate for a moment with his fork raised, and she realized he was breathing in the intoxicating aroma of the food she had just spooned onto his plate.

"You will take over the cooking, won't you Katie?" he said.

Katie paused, deliberately, just before she replied. No harm in making him sweat, just a little. The children looked up at her with anxious faces, all waiting to hear her reply, eager for a reassurance that she wouldn't be hanging up her apron and catching the four-thirty to London.

"If that's what you want, sir," she said, at last.

A loud cheer went up around the table, the children expressing their approval by stamping their feet and banging their cutlery on the table, and Katie felt a little surge of triumph.

The food must have put Michael in a good mood, because after dinner he announced that he needed the children to "help" him operate the gramophone player.

"You got a gramophone?" Roy asked, dark eyes glinting with interest. "A good one? And records to play on it?"

"The best money can buy," Michael said, matter-of-factly.

A whoop of delight went up, and the children swarmed around him to wheel him off to the library.

Katie did the dishes in the scullery, listening to soft strains of music carrying from the other room. She thought she heard Artie Shaw's wicked clarinet, followed by Harry James—sinful on the saxophone—playing the most suggestive version of "You Made Me Love You" that she had ever heard. Just the sound of that music made her cheeks flame. So seductive.

She decided to leave the dishes to drain, so she could go listen to the music properly. She stood in the doorway of the library and watched them at work. Roy selected the records, showing them first to Michael for approval, then little Alfie put them on the turntable and operated the needle so they didn't get scratched. The twins took up their positions in the middle of the red turkey carpet, and danced like there was no tomorrow.

The children liked the lively ones best, but Katie loved it when they played the sultry dance music. It made her think of big smoky ballrooms and the thrill of being in the arms of a man that you liked.

"Come and sit down," Michael suggested gently, indicating the place on the old leather chesterfield near him.

She felt a bit shy, but she crossed the room and perched herself on the couch. He handed her a heavy gramophone record to inspect. She slid it out of its brown paper sleeve, and turned it around so she could read the title. *Glenn Miller – Fools Rush In Where Angels Fear to Tread.* The song she had wanted to play on her very first day—the day his lordship found her exploring the place on her own. He had noticed. He had remembered.

"Ladies choice," Michael announced. Katie looked up and caught the amusement in those cool blue eyes of his. Would she ever be done blushing if he kept looking at her like that?

He must have sensed her embarrassment, because his lips quirked into the faintest hint of a smile.

"What's it to be, then Katie?"

# Chapter Six

The next morning, Katie came running when she heard his lordship calling out from his bedroom on the ground floor.

"What is it, sir? Are you hurt?"

He was lying back against his pillows, looking languidly handsome as ever, but his face wore a scowl. "No, but I bloody well will be if I can't get you to answer the bell. I've been ringing for the last forty minutes."

"I'm sorry. I've been seeing the boys off to school. There was an urgent crisis involving Roy's spelling book."

"Are you free now?" he demanded. He flicked disconsolately at his bed sheets, and began to push them aside. He wore only a white cotton undershirt and a pair of stripy pajama trousers.

"Yes, I am." Katie knew she should look away as his lordship maneuvered himself to the edge of the bed, hauling first one leg and then the other with his hands until he was sitting on the edge of the mattress. He had long, slim legs, obviously wasted from six months lack of use. The pajama trousers were loose and baggy on him.

He stopped. He glanced up at her with reluctance and uncertainty in his blue eyes. A hint of color crept across the lean angles of his face.

"The thing is, Katie, until yesterday I always had someone to help me in the mornings with getting dressed and finding things, you know . . . "

"Mrs. Jessop, you mean."

"Yes. We had a routine."

Katie felt a pang of guilt. Michael needed help, he was not quite as independent as he liked to pretend, and faithful old Jessop used to play along with it all. Katie had deprived Michael of help that he desperately needed.

"Where shall I start?" Katie said, mentally rolling up her sleeves. "You want me to wheel you into the bathroom? Shall I help you to wash?"

"God, Katie, I'd rather die than ask you to do this."

"I think I can understand that," she said. "But dying isn't on the agenda today, sir, so I guess we'll both have to grit our teeth."

He smiled, but he was still reluctant.

Katie sat down beside him. "Are you taking this off, or what?" she said, tugging at the front of the white undershirt.

Michael looked sheepish. He ran a hand through the fronds of blond hair that fell down over his forehead. He shoved them out of the way, like a shy teenager waiting to undress for the school nurse.

"S'pose so," he muttered, hauling off the garment so that he was naked to the waist.

Katie's gaze fluttered shyly over the fine contours of his torso. It was all she could do to stifle the soft murmur that almost escaped her lips. He was beautiful, no question about it, though she felt she had no right to admire him. She felt her face flush with shame.

"This isn't going to be easy, is it?" Michael said, meeting her gaze. His candid blue eyes were even more disarming than his beautiful, beautiful chest.

"No," whispered Katie.

His fingers lingered nervously on the waistband that rode low on his narrow hips. She wasn't sure if he truly meant to remove his pants, but she decided she wasn't staying to find out.

"Hot water and a towel!" she blurted and ran from the room like the place was on fire.

*

Katie thought the flaming embarrassment that reddened her face would never go away. All morning she thought about his lordship. Surely, it wasn't possible that she could have *those* kinds of feelings for a man again. And what about the look she thought she saw in his eyes last night? Did she misread that? Surely, his condition meant he couldn't . . .

Curse him and his bedroom eyes! She tried to concentrate on making steak and kidney pudding for lunch, and she had flour all over her hands when Alfie came rushing in through the back door.

"Come and see, Miss Rafferty," Alfie hopped up and down in excitement.

Katie hoped he wasn't about to wet himself. "See what?"

"See what we found in the stables!" Alfie tried to pull on Katie's arm. "You have to see!"

He was a sweet boy and he rarely asked her for anything, so Katie felt obliged to leave what she was doing. She smiled and untied her apron, leaving it hanging over the back of a kitchen chair.

Alfie beamed a big, gappy grin. "It'll be worth the effort, Miss, I promise." He took hold of her hand and hauled her out through the kitchen door. They walked briskly down the path and turned the corner to look across the drive.

And there it was. A bright red sports car—an MG Roadster, or something like it; Katie wasn't very good at recognizing cars. It was long and low with an open top. At present, it had a towrope attached to the front bumper, and it was being hauled along by Roy and the twins, with much hysterical laughter and a certain amount of swearing.

Sitting in it, like a rajah, was his lordship, wearing his flying goggles and a brown leather helmet. "Tally ho!" he cried. "Chocks away!"

It was quite a sight, and definitely worth taking her apron off for.

Alfie ran to lend his weight to the task, though he wasn't much help by the looks of things. They were doing at least thirty inches an hour.

"What in the blue blazes is this?" said Katie, trying to suppress her laughter. Michael tooted the horn enthusiastically when he saw her and ordered the children to stop by the steps.

"Isn't this great?" he asked. "Haven't taken the old girl out for a spin in ages. I used to drive her everywhere before the war. We're going to the front hedge and back. Haven't seen the front hedge for a while, either. Want to come?"

"No!" she said. "I'll weigh you down."

Michael took off the goggles and removed the helmet. He tossed them over his shoulder so he could make a more direct appeal.

"You know you want to!" he said, with a ravishing smile.

Seeing him sitting there in his car, she caught a glimpse of the devil-may-care young man that he had once been. Strands of straight fair hair fell forward and shone gold in the sunlight. He flashed her a confident grin and leaned across to open the passenger door for her.

This was a man who was rarely refused, she thought. A man who liked fast cars and fast women. *A man she rather liked the look of.* Instantly she tried to dispel that thought.

He patted the seat beside him, "Come for a spin!"

Katie gazed longingly at the car. She'd never in her life been in a car like that, with a man like that.

She weakened and climbed in. The car had luxurious red leather seats—real leather with a soft, buttery feel. She closed the passenger door carefully, and it clicked shut.

"Where are you taking me, then?"

"Told you, Front Hedge. After that, I don't know. Maybe we could go for a drink at the Dog and Whistle."

Roy gave a kind of angry roar from his position hauling the rope at the front. "I ain't pulling you all the way to the ruddy Dog and Whistle, Mister. This thing is twice as heavy since she got in."

"Thank you very much," Katie retorted. "Actually, I'm sure I've lost a bit of weight since I came to this wonderful country of yours."

"Come on, Roy, put your back into it! We've slowed to a snail's pace!"

The boys concerted their efforts. They gave a last desperate tug on the rope and hauled with all their might, but the car wouldn't budge. In the end, someone must have lost their grip on the rope and they all tumbled into a heap on the driveway. There were shrieks of laughter and howls of outrage as the four got up, pushing and shoving one another.

Katie smiled sweetly at Michael. "Not quite enough horsepower, my lord." She began to unfasten the passenger door. "I'd better get back to the kitchen, sir, and finish the cooking. The kids will have a hearty appetite after all this, and Mrs. Mallory's coming to check up on us all."

"Crikey. Marjory Mallory for lunch today?"

"She's not on the menu, sir. That's steak and kidney pie. But she's arriving at twelve o'clock sharp."

Michael smiled. "I expect she is. She's a stickler for punctuality."

Katie stepped lightly out of the car, and although she didn't know what possessed her, she turned and blew Michael a kiss. He returned it with a flourish and another glorious, sunny smile.

"Come on, team. Tally ho," he said, to encourage the children to pick up the rope and try again. "Chocks away!"

*

Michael toyed with his portion of boiled cabbage until he noticed Mrs. Mallory was giving him one of her disapproving stares.

"Waste not, want not, Michael," she mouthed at him, almost silently.

He sighed and forked it in. The pie had been divine, of course, one of Katie's culinary triumphs, but he didn't care for boiled cabbage. He could never quite forgive a cabbage for being so . . . cabbagey.

Katie had served the lunch in the main dining room, since they had company. Michael had worried that the wheelchair wouldn't fit under the giant polished oval table, but it did. Mrs. Mallory appeared very jolly, and she ate a formidable quantity of steak and kidney pie. She was wearing a dress today—a sort of giant, blue tent- instead of her uniform. Michael still couldn't work out why she was here. Mrs. Mallory was the kind of woman who always visited people with a specific purpose in mind, and usually it involved bullying them into doing something virtuous for the community or for the war. But today, she hadn't yet revealed her true purpose.

"You've done very well, my dear," Mrs. Mallory said to Katie. "No wonder the children are so settled."

Michael glanced around at the children. Perhaps she was just checking up on the little devils. They looked deceptively angelic today with their hair combed flat with water and their faces scrubbed clean. They were so quiet and subdued, as if they imagined Mrs. Mallory held the power of life and death in her hands on the sheer force of having been the billeting officer.

"I think the whole village is a little curious about Katie," Mrs. Mallory said. "You know how rumors fly."

"Yes I do," Michael agreed. "The rumors flew sky high after Katie sacked Mrs. Jessop."

Alfie giggled. "There was a lady in the village shop saying that Katie and Mrs. Jessop had a wrestling match on the sitting room carpet."

"People do tend to exaggerate, dear. I hope you set them straight." Mrs. Mallory indicated that she'd like a third helping of the pie, and Katie handed her the spoon.

Alfie smiled to himself. "I told them I didn't actually see it, but I heard that Mrs. Jessop went bright purple."

"Purple with rage?" said Mrs. Mallory in an amused tone. "That doesn't sound like Lizzie. Whatever did you say to her, Katie dear?"

"It was over the ration books. It had become obvious that—"

Michael felt he had to intervene. "Katie, you must understand, I will probably need to reinstate Mrs. Jessop."

Various cries of dismay went up all around the table. Katie looked at Michael, the questions clear in her eyes.

"Not to do the cooking," he hastened to add, "but to help me, and to help with the rest of the housework. You can't do it all."

Katie looked relieved. "No, perhaps not. But the woman is *dishonest*, sir."

"Sshhh. She's not dishonest," Michael tried hard to communicate with only his eyes that he wanted Katie to shut up. She looked as if she would argue with him, but then she glanced sideways at Mrs. Mallory and then said nothing.

"As I say, she's not dishonest. She's been on the staff here for over thirty years, and she has always made a valuable contribution."

Katie rolled her eyes.

"Lizzie Jessop is the last of the servants who were here in your parents' day, isn't she, Michael?"

"Yes. Exactly," said Michael. "Jessop is a tradition we must uphold. I'm planning to talk to her tomorrow, if I get the chance. Try to smooth things over."

"Good idea, Michael." Mrs. Mallory sat back in her well-padded dining chair and folded her hands over her enormous girth. Perhaps she was finally full, Michael thought, ungraciously.

"Well, as I was saying, people in the village are very curious about Katie. They'd love to meet her. And of course they'd love to see more of you, Michael, now that you are feeling better. The village dance is coming up next month."

Michael sighed. Mrs. Mallory's purpose was about to become clear.

"The dance has been held on May Day for at least the last two hundred years," she said. "It is impossible that you have forgotten."

Michael glanced at Katie and noticed that a pink flush of embarrassment was coloring her cheeks rather prettily. She moistened her lips and looked down at her table napkin, refusing to meet his eye.

"The dance seems a marvelous opportunity for Katie to meet everyone in the village, wouldn't you say?"

"Absolutely. I hope she enjoys it very much," Michael said, rather crossly.

Mrs. Mallory wasn't giving up that easily. "And what about *you*, Michael?"

"What the hell would I do at a dance, Marjory? Except drink myself stupid and chat to the vicar?"

Four children looked up sharply, their eyes wide.

"Your parents always made the effort to attend. And you yourself were talking about upholding tradition, just a few minutes ago."

George piped up. "You could invite Mrs. Jessop, if you think no one else will go with you," he said, in a helpful tone of voice.

"Dear God," Michael said, under his breath. This was too much.

"Blasphemy. In front of the children," Katie murmured.

Michael gave them what he hoped was a withering glance.

"You should consider attending the dance, Michael," Mrs. Mallory persisted. It's a duty that comes with your title, like attending the House of Lords, although I understand you've been shirking that responsibility, too."

Michael sighed deeply. "You know I can't bear sitting in the House, Marjory."

"He can't bear sitting anywhere—he's always saying so," said Roy. It was the first of Roy's usual tactless interjections at the meal, and Michael was grateful it was such a mild one.

Alfie's eyes were almost out on stalks at the mention of the House of Lords. He leaned forward across the table, and said "Hey, Mister, have you ever met the king?"

"On several occasions. Though he doesn't usually attend the village dance."

Mrs. Mallory gave a snort of impatience. "Think it over, Michael. Think about what your father would have done."

Michael thought for a moment and then he smiled. "I think if my father had taken Katie Rafferty to the dance, my mother would have slapped his face and banished him to the billiard room for a fortnight."

"Michael!"

Katie had obviously had enough. She stood up and started clearing away the plates, none too graciously. When she snatched Michael's plate, a drop of gravy landed on his sleeve. He scowled down at it, and then glanced up and saw her face reddening with alarm. He reached languidly for his napkin and dabbed away the spot.

She looked visibly relieved. "Shall I be serving the pudding, now, sir?"

For a moment, Michael felt contrite. It wasn't her fault that she was caught in the crossfire between him and Mrs. Mallory. But really, he *couldn't* take a servant to the dance, not even one as pretty as Katie.

After lunch, they moved to the drawing room at Mrs. Mallory's insistence. Michael knew what the wretched woman was trying to do: force a motley group of people with nothing in common to pretend they were a real family. He scowled at the woman, but he let her have her way. For the moment, at least.

Michael hoped to ignore everyone and gaze out of the window, but Alfie tugged at his sleeve.

"I've got an idea about the car, sir."

Michael leaned forward and whispered to the boy, "Spill."

"Roy told me that people in London siphon petrol out of other people's tanks if they need some."

Michael frowned, and glanced across at Roy who was sitting stiffly on the chesterfield next to Mrs. Mallory, receiving a grilling about something or other.

Alfie's chattering revealed a keen interest in the physics involved in siphoning petrol. Michael was beginning to get the impression that Alfie was a boffin in a child's body, one of those midget geniuses that some unlucky parents discovered in their otherwise normal families.

Michael's physics was a little rusty, so he couldn't really help Alfie. Michael had been a classical scholar at Cambridge, and a disinterested one at that. His chief talent had been attracting pretty girls to go punting with him, on the river. Michael had been an expert at handling the shallow watercraft—and handling the girls who liked to recline in them. He could see them now, trailing their fingers in the water and enjoying the afternoon sun. He sighed. Those days were gone.

He realized Alfie was trying to ask him something.

"Sorry, what did you say?"

"Should I ask Roy to siphon some petrol for you, Mister Lord? Then you could really take the MG for a spin."

"Heavens no! Roy will get into trouble if he does something like that," Michael lowered his voice so that Katie and Mrs. Mallory couldn't hear. "Roy mustn't do that. Under any circumstances."

"Will you ask Mr. Hammond, then? He must get a petrol allowance for the farm, I reckon."

Michael shrugged. "I'm not sure. He's always driving around in the Austin. He must get the petrol from somewhere."

"If he's got plenty, he could give us some, couldn't he? I'd love to see that car of yours going, sir. The engine in a roadster does over five thousand revolutions a minute." Alfie was a mine of useless information.

Michael smiled. He'd love to see the MG going again, too, especially when he remembered Katie's pretty face flushing with pleasure when she got into the passenger seat. "I think I will telephone Mr. Hammond. That's a good idea."

Perhaps there was a petrol allowance, Michael wondered, for running the farm vehicles and taking stock to market. And if it were true, Hammond was making full use of it. He was always borrowing the Austin and taking girls out on little jaunts. Yes, he envied Hammond. Not only did the bloke have two fully functional legs, he also had the confidence of a man about three times more attractive than he actually was. All that man had to do was start talking and twenty minutes later, all the village lasses were like putty in his hands. If Michael didn't do something about it, he'd be all over Katie.

Michael wondered how Hammond had escaped the war. He seemed perfectly fit and healthy. Perhaps he was exempt because of the farm. Michael had never been remotely interested in the details. His father had handled it all until his recent death. All Michael knew was that Hammond was allowed to stay and the other men had all been drafted. These days, the farm was worked by three conscientious objectors and a land girl.

His curiosity roused, Michael abruptly left the gathering to wheel his way to his office, where he telephoned Hammond straight away. He reckoned the boy was right. Maybe there was a petrol allowance.

# Chapter Seven

"Has anyone asked you to the dance yet?" Mrs. Mallory inquired when she joined Katie in the queue at the butcher's shop.

"Oh yes," Katie replied and rolled her eyes. "You'd never think there was a shortage of men in this village. I wish people would stop asking me. "

"And is one of them Michael, may I ask?" A glint came into Mrs. Mallory's eye.

"Michael?"

"His lordship."

"I know his lordship's name is Michael, but he won't ask me. He can't dance. He doesn't like music, and he doesn't like me. Three very good reasons why he won't ask."

"I was hoping he would."

"I'm going with Arthur Perkins. The policeman. At least he's polite."

"Oh, I am disappointed, Katie. I thought it would be a chance to get Michael out of the house. He used to love the village dance, and it would be a chance to show people that he's back in charge now, to begin to win people's love and loyalty like his parents did. Tell Arthur you've changed your mind."

"I'm shocked you would even suggest such a thing," Katie said, but she kept her tone of voice light and good-humored. "Arthur would be very disappointed."

"I know. But I think someone else may feel a little put out when he realizes he's missed his chance. And it wouldn't be cricket to change horses now, would it?"

"You're mixing your metaphors, Mrs. Mallory."

Katie smiled, struggling with the image of Arthur and Michael as rival mounts. Arthur Perkins, the village policeman, was a bit of a pit pony with his wispy brown hair and his tubby underbelly. Michael was pure English Thoroughbred—refined, highly strung, and immaculately groomed. The type of animal you longed to reach out and touch to see if it was really as warm and smooth and handsome as it looked. Yes, she knew which one she liked best, even if she only admitted it to herself.

Then she bit her lip and experienced a wave of guilt. Surely, it wasn't right to have even a hint of *that* kind of feeling for a man like Michael. His injuries made it highly inappropriate. On the other hand, if you were lucky enough to work for a rich, handsome, young man you'd be almost bound to have secret dreams. If the man expressed interest in you it would be a huge temptation, but still one best avoided. Affairs between employers and servants went on all the time, Katie knew, but they nearly always ended in disgrace for the girl. She knew all about that, and Tom had only been a grocer's son.

Heaven knows, she didn't want a man, anyway. She'd only agreed to go to the dance with Arthur because he wouldn't stop asking her until she said yes.

*

She aroused him. Every time she was near, Michael thought about what he would have done if he had been on his feet. The flirtatious little jokes he would have told just to see if his interest was reciprocated, and the moves he would have made if it were. He would have crept up on her working in the kitchen and tried to steal a kiss. Her reaction would have been priceless. He would show her around the estate, impressing her with his rank and privilege before shocking her a little with an invitation to the hayloft to enjoy a *spectacular* view.

That was all over now. He could see the years stretching out in front of him while he sat like this, miserable and aloof, until he became old and hunched. If he ever did take a wife, he supposed it would be a platonic arrangement; he'd find a woman who wanted to marry him for his title and they would live like a pair of amiable neighbors, enjoying quiet breakfasts on the terrace and polite but distant conversation.

*God, that wasn't what he wanted!*

He'd rather have nothing than endure that. Before his accident, he'd been such a passionate man. He *loved* the company of women and had no trouble getting it, either. He always had a girlfriend. And then there was Connie—blond, statuesque Connie—of whom his parents had thought so highly. Though they didn't really know her, not like Michael did. She was a superficial person, difficult to fathom at first, hiding her true feelings underneath her languid good manners. Her people were richer than the Farrendens, and since his family was extremely wealthy, that made her the catch of the century. It had been a consummate triumph when she agreed to marry him, and his parents had been so thrilled.

They never knew about his accident and how it had all fallen apart with Connie. It was a kind of comfort that they died thinking he would marry a fine girl and take over the estate when he came back—victorious, of course—from the war.

But then the nagging doubts came. Is that what his parents thought? They must have been worried out of their minds while he flew sorties every day for the RAF. They had followed the war news with great anxiety, both of them having lived through the first one. They clutched at each other's hands and told each other it would be over soon. And it was, for them.

They had been returning from London in their car just after the blackout was enforced in earnest. Using car headlamps was forbidden and they shouldn't have attempted the journey at all. They lost their way in the dark, which was understandable since the road signs had all been removed.

Michael sighed. They must have gotten flustered and tried to get back onto the right road. Michael's father was already dead at the scene. His mother died three days later in hospital. So he had survived and they had died. Needlessly.

He'd toyed with the idea of joining them. Thought about finding his father's old rifle and doing the deed himself. But his mother would be disgusted by such cowardice. She would tell him that option neglected his duty to his tenants and to the villagers whose loyalties belonged to him. Four centuries of tradition abandoned because he didn't want to buck up and run the estate as he had been born and bred to do.

There was no easy way out.

# Chapter Eight

Scraping the plates in the scullery, Katie was glad the meal had gone as well as it did. Empty plates meant they had enjoyed it, and just for today, she left the stack of dishes on the draining board for later. She went back into the warm kitchen to listen to the wireless. Michael was still there, of course, notwithstanding everything he had said about needing to write important letters in the peace and quiet of his study. Katie had come to realize that lately his lordship spent most of his time in the part of the house that used to be called "below stairs."

Alfie was just coming back from some childish mission of his own, and he had a look of great importance on his face as he crossed the room to speak to Michael. He leaned across the arm of the wheelchair as if they were old school pals.

"Mr. Hammond has arrived with the petrol, sir," Alfie said, conspiratorially.

Katie heard him. "What's all this?"

Michael beamed at her, boyishly. "I'd like you to step out onto the front drive with me. I've a little surprise for you."

So the three of them trooped outside. Or at least, Katie trooped, and Alfie trooped. Michael's wheels rolled noiselessly across the hall and down the ramp onto the front terrace.

Hammond was outside fussing over the MG. Beside it sat two metal petrol cans he had brought up from the farm. He raised his cap when he saw Katie.

"Afternoon, miss," he said, and he gave Michael a wary, respectful nod. Clearly, Hammond did not intend to be quite so familiar today, not with his lordship about.

"Did you start her?" Michael called out.

"Not yet, sir, I thought you'd like to have a try."

"Very considerate of you, Hammond." Michael smiled. "Give

me a hand to get behind the wheel, will you?"

Hammond leaped to the terrace to help move Michael, bumping the chair down the shallow steps that led down to the front drive.

Michael hauled himself up out of the wheelchair and across into the front seat of the car, easing himself in behind the steering wheel. He pressed the starter and the engine fluttered and died.

"Katie, this is where you come in. Come here and sit on my knee."

"Sir! I shall do no such thing! That would be most improper!"

"Well sit next to me then, there's almost room for two. I need you to help me drive the car."

Katie was horrified.

"It's an order, Katie. I have urgent supplies to collect in the village."

She shook her head. "If it's all that urgent, send Hammond."

"I have never let Hammond drive this car and I don't intend to start now."

"I'm only allowed the old Austin, Miss," Hammond chipped in, jovially. "That and the tractor, coz it only does about five mile an hour. His lordship don't trust me with the MG."

"Having experienced your driving once, Mr. Hammond, I can see why."

"Katie! Stop gossiping with Hammond and come here, would you!"

She must have put too much brandy in the sauce that they'd had with their pudding, because she did exactly as he asked. She went over to the driver's door and squeezed herself into the seat beside him.

"I hope I didn't tread on your feet," she said, acutely aware of being squashed against Michael. The fabric of his gray tweed suit felt slightly rough against her bare legs, and she smelled a subtle masculine fragrance—some expensive type of aftershave, perhaps.

"I don't suppose I'd feel it you did," he said, and she caught the echo of regret in his voice.

It was certainly a tight fit with both of them in the driver's seat, but he didn't seem to mind. He put his arm around her and tested to see if he could still reach the steering wheel. He waggled it from side to side and seemed satisfied. He was smiling again now. Settled this close, Katie noticed a hint of fair stubble along his jaw-line where he had shaved a little unevenly.

"Now I'm going to press the starter button, and when I do, I want you to put your foot on the accelerator and give it a nice little squeeze."

Katie shrugged. "I can't drive."

"I'm driving. You are providing the impetus, that's all."

"The what?"

"The impetus."

Katie laughed. "What the . . . "

"Don't argue. Just squeeze the pedal when I say so."

His slim, elegant fingers were on the starter button and she did what he told her to do. The car rumbled into life, and Michael gave an excited cheer. Even Hammond looked rather pleased. "She's humming like a bird, sir!"

"She is indeed."

Alfie was hopping up and down on the terrace. "Are you going to drive her, for real?"

"We certainly are! Tell the others we'll be back in half an hour."

"Half an hour!" Katie exclaimed. "Where are you taking me?"

"I told you: urgent supplies."

Katie was laughing now, happy and elated.

"Keep squeezing," Michael instructed.

This time, to her surprise, the car hopped into life.

"Sorry," he said. "I slipped her into gear while you weren't looking. Have another go, gently this time or we'll go straight through the front hedge."

Before long they had the rhythm worked out. He steered and she pushed the accelerator as the car rumbled down the drive and out through the front gates.

"Freedom!" he cried as they hit the open road, still urging her to keep up the acceleration. She screamed as they took a bend in the road a little faster than she was expecting. She felt her whole body thrown against Michael's as they rounded the curve.

It was exhilarating. It was magic. He kept yelling at her to press harder. She screamed with laughter as he steered the car in a slalom pattern along the middle of the road.

"You'll get us killed!" she said.

"No, I won't."

She couldn't help it; she surrendered to the delirious feeling of excitement, to the pleasure of this reckless ride. Perhaps it wasn't as dangerous as it looked, she reasoned. There wasn't any traffic on the road.

"Yes!" Michael cried. He sailed through the village, yelling like a young hooligan, to the astonishment of various villagers quietly going about their business. They hardly expected to see "his lordship, poor man" whizzing along in his red car, with a girl at his side on this fine April Saturday.

Katie gasped as Michael wheeled the car around and pulled into the forecourt at the Dog and Whistle. The pub was thronging with people.

"Brakes!" he demanded, and she stabbed at them sharply.

The roadster squealed to a halt, and Michael beeped the horn in a very high-handed fashion.

"Come out, Mr. Roebuck, and take our orders!"

Katie slapped Michael's arm, playfully. "Don't order him around as if you owned the place.

"But I do. Own the place, that is."

"You're kidding. The Dog and Whistle?"

"That's right. He pays rent on it, most of the time."

The landlord appeared at the door and Michael called out for the best bitter and a glass of lemonade. There was no question of going inside with the wheelchair abandoned on the drive back at Farrenden Manor.

"I suppose these are your urgent supplies?" Katie asked.

"They are."

Michael smiled at her, eyes twinkling. He sipped his beer with a look of triumph on his face.

# Chapter Nine

Sunday morning Katie heard Michael's bell jangle twice while she was hurrying to prepare a breakfast tray. She popped a fresh napkin beside his butter knife, lifted the tray, and hurried down the corridor in the direction of his room.

He was sitting up on his four-poster bed, wearing only his pajama trousers. His feet were bare. Even his feet were long, slim and elegant. He was reading something, studying the pages with interest.

Katie found the sight of his bare arms rather distracting, too—they were curved and well-muscled from transferring himself in and out of the chair all the time.

"Come and look at this," he said eagerly.

"What about your breakfast, sir?"

To her dismay, Michael dismissed the breakfast tray with a wave of his hand. Katie moved a few things to make room on his dressing table and noticed for the first time a photograph of Michael with a young woman. A posed photo, but a happy one, taken to mark a special occasion. Michael was looking very dashing in his uniform and the young lady at his side was a radiant blonde with a perfect coiffure and a wide, triumphant smile.

"Who's this?" Katie asked and picked it up.

Michael's face showed barely a flicker of emotion. "Oh, that's Connie. Ancient history. Stick it in my sock drawer if you like. I want you to take a look at this!"

"What happened to her, sir, if you don't mind me asking?"

"She ditched me, Katie. After my accident. I don't want to talk about it. Least said, soonest mended."

Oh yes, Katie knew all about not talking about the past.

She left the photograph and came over to stand beside the bed.

Michael held out a pamphlet he'd been reading about back injuries that claimed that with regular exercise, a man could relearn the art of walking after a serious injury.

"Fascinating, isn't it?"

Katie gave him a weak smile. "Perhaps it's aimed at people convalescing from less drastic injuries than your own."

He ignored her completely. "I think it's advice worth taking. I've got crutches—they're in the wardrobe."

"You've got crutches, sir?" She was surprised, for though his upper body was strong and powerful, his legs looked much too frail to manage on a pair of crutches. "Did the hospital give them to you?"

"No. I ordered them myself. Dr. Larchwood from the village authorized it."

"Did Dr. Larchwood think it was safe for you to use them?"

"He wasn't wildly optimistic. Doctors never are, especially stuck-in-the-mud, pedestrian, village doctors like him. But I wanted them, and he agreed that it would be a good idea to have them for when the time was right. I'd like to try them out."

"Do you want me to ask Dr. Larchwood to come and see you? Just to make sure that the time *is* right?"

"No. Of course not. I'll be the judge of that. Today I feel like I could do it. Open the wardrobe door and get the crutches."

She sighed and went over to the enormous piece of furniture made of polished walnut, with a pair of doors that looked like the entrance to a barn. She opened the right hand door and moved some of his clothes aside looking for the crutches, breathing in the slightly masculine scent that lingered among his garments. The crutches were standing at the back, along with Michael's cricket pads and an old tennis racket.

He heaved himself across the bed and moved his legs across with his hands, arranging them so that he was sitting on the edge of the bed. Through the thin fabric of his trousers, his legs looked like giraffe legs, long and spindly, and Katie felt sure they couldn't possibly support him. But she forced herself to remain silent.

"Hand me my crutches. I need to know the worst."

"Not today!" she blurted out. "It's too soon, sir. I could put these in a safe place, and you could try another day." *Not today. Don't let him try today.* She didn't want to see him fail.

"Do as I ask."

Reluctantly she placed a crutch on either side of him, and he struggled to position them under his arms. He made a feeble attempt to hoist himself up, but he was nervous and wary.

"Please," he said, looking up at her with vulnerable, blue eyes. "Can you help me?"

"Of course," she said. She'd never had such a terrible sense of foreboding. She took away one of the crutches, ducked under his arm, and prepared to take the weight of his whole body.

"Ready?" he said.

"Ready," she answered. "One, two, three!"

He gave a cry of pain as they rose unsteadily to their feet. Katie struggled to keep him upright.

She glanced up and gave him a desperate smile of encouragement. Beads of sweat were forming on his forehead. His face was as white as the bed sheets.

He clutched her shoulder with the tightness of desperation. "It's nice to stand beside you," he said, but his face showed terrible strain.

She knew exactly the moment when he gave up the impossible struggle. His legs crumpled up awkwardly beneath him, the useless crutch splayed out across the bedroom floor, and they both crashed to the floor. Katie was flung against the edge of the bed, and Michael cried out in pain and frustration.

She thought her heart would break in two at that sound.

Katie's wrist was sore and she had ruined her stockings. Michael flung away the wooden crutch in anger and frustration, hearing it crash against the dressing table legs. His head went down in despair.

"Michael, don't!" She didn't think she could bear to see him cry. She moved nearer, and tried to touch his arm.

She wanted to touch the nape of his neck where his honey colored hair had been cut short. She wanted to do something, *anything*, before he let vent to his grief. Determined to console him, Katie impulsively tilted his face to hers, and kissed him hard. Her mouth locked onto his with a desperate, crazy yearning not to see him vanquished. Her hands cupped his face as she continued to press her mouth on his, ignoring any signs of surprise.

She felt a ripple of movement and a response—a passionate, masculine response. She felt the pressure of his lips on hers, and his tongue searching and finding hers. His kiss was wild and desperate, and it was everything she'd secretly imagined. She gave a soft moan and let a powerful wave of sensation wash over her.

He seemed encouraged by that sound and he kissed her again and again, one kiss melting into another. Soon she realized that his arms were around her, and his fingers were tangled in her hair.

"Katie," he said, and opened his blue eyes to look at her. His face was a portrait of astonished rapture.

Consumed with regret and embarrassment, Katie put her hands up to her face. "Forgive me, sir, forgive me!"

"It's all right," he said, and his blue eyes spoke of a new understanding between them.

"It isn't! It was a dreadful liberty I took. Please sir, I only meant to take your mind off what happened."

"You did," he said, and he smiled at her. He put a finger to his own mouth, just where her lips had been, and then he reached out and touched her lips with his fingertips. He seemed to be in a state of dazed amazement.

"I didn't stop to think," Katie said, in a scared whisper. "I only did it so you wouldn't be so sad!"

"It's all right, Katie. Really. You meant to be kind—and it was extraordinary." He struggled to reposition himself, dragging at his useless legs with his left hand. "Help me up, now, my love. I should like to get up off the floor."

"Of course, of course!" She flustered around him, getting him onto the edge of the bed. The "my love" slip filled her with guilt.

"You must be cold, sir," she said to cover her flailing emotions. She could hardly look him in the eye, but she found his pajama top and began doing the buttons up for him, as if he was one of the children. He placed a hand over hers.

"It was a good kiss," he said, and gave her a direct, penetrating look. "We'll share another one some time, won't we?"

She couldn't answer him. He looked so hopeful, just as he had desperately hoped for a full recovery, and she felt like such a fraud. She would have to tell him that it was all a terrible mistake. She pulled her hand away from his and stood up.

"Please, sir. You must ask Mrs. Jessop to come back and help you. I'll apologize to her myself if you want. Or you could hire a proper nurse. I'm so sorry!"

Michael almost laughed at her. "Katie. I don't want a bloody nurse, and I don't want Jessop. I want you."

Katie shook her head, baffled by her own emotions, confused by the strength of her feelings for him. "Things were bad enough before, sir, when it was all inside me. Now it's a thousand times worse."

Then she turned and fled from the room.

# Chapter Ten

Michael tackled his paperwork with renewed energy. Normally the thought of several hours of farm administration would have filled him with gloom, but today, he felt as if he had a spring in his step—or at least in his fountain pen.

He paid half a dozen overdue bills, writing out large checks as if he were a great philanthropist. He canceled his subscription to the tennis club and made his apologies to the Young Farmers Association, all without the usual surge of anger and resentment that accompanied thinking about people who were fit and well and didn't have to spend their lives sitting down.

She's delightful, he thought. Very pretty, and very sweet—but oh so emotional. Her kiss stirred sensations he had only dreamed of feeling again. He leaned back in his chair and for the first time since the accident, he thought about the future and making plans for the farm—that is, when he could stop himself from daydreaming about that amazing kiss.

He was just writing an apology to the coal man for the delay in settling his account when he heard her footsteps on the path outside his window. He'd know the sound of her light, determined step anywhere. He looked up and was stunned to see her suitcase in hand.

Michael didn't need to think. Quick as a flash, he wheeled the chair around and headed back through his own rooms to the ramp that led to the front garden. His hands worked the wheels of the chair faster than ever, but by the time he arrived at the front of the house, Katie was already walking down the drive, heading purposefully toward the gates.

"Katie!"

Her reddish brown curls blew back in the wind, and she seemed to falter, but she pretended not to hear him. He noticed that in her haste to get out of his house, she hadn't even put on her hat, though she was usually very correct about that sort of thing.

"Katie!"

He worked the wheels faster, thanking God that he hadn't been able to get new gravel for the drive. He could get the chair scudding along at a fast clip in the dirt, and the drive's downward slope helped tremendously. He must look ridiculous in hot pursuit of a pretty girl in a bloody wheelchair, but his fear of losing her was greater than his pride.

"Katie! Katie! Stop and turn around this minute!" Michael shouted. He had felt happy this morning, in a way he had never expected to feel happy again. Happy, on a day when he had resigned himself to the bloody chair. Happy, because of this little Irish wench. This extraordinary girl who provoked him and challenged him and made him feel alive again. He wasn't about to let her slip through his fingers.

"There isn't a train for two hours at least," he lied. He was encouraged to see that slowed Katie a little.

She was nearly at the gatehouse when he caught up with her. He was rather out of breath from working the wheels so hard, and the chair was spattered with mud.

"Oh, sir," she sighed, turning to face him, with a look of hurt resignation in her eyes.

"What's all this?" he demanded, gesturing imperiously at the offending brown suitcase.

She glanced down at it, and looked guilty. "It's better that I leave."

"Better for whom?" he said. "Me? The children? Jessop, maybe? She's probably the only one who won't be sorry to see the back of you, Irish troublemaker that you are."

Katie clenched her teeth and didn't reply.

"Where on earth will you go?"

"I can't bear it now," she said. "I can't keep working for you with all of this inside my head, and my heart."

"Your heart?" he said, and he looked up at her with a hint of a smile. "Surely, you're not afraid you might fall in love with me?"

She flashed him a sudden guilty look while a scarlet blush flamed on her cheeks. "I'll not let that happen to me again."

He grinned. His money and his looks had often given him the confidence to be candid. It amused him to see the effect his startling remarks had on people, and it had often paid off. *She had as good as admitted it!*

He was triumphant, but he spoke gently to her. "Katie, look at me."

She did so, reluctantly.

"Do you have any idea what it means to me," he said, "that you could even imagine yourself in love with me as I am now?"

"No," she said, simply. "But I can surely imagine how it will all end, sir."

She surprised him. He had spent a pleasant morning trying to consider where it might lead. Apparently her thoughts were not quite along the same lines, for she was close to tears, he realized.

"I must go," she said.

"Katie," he said softly, and tried to take her hand. She shied away, but he could see her softening, regretting, weakening in her resolve to leave him. The suitcase fell from her hand and toppled over flat in the driveway. She let it lie where it fell, and stood there brushing away the tears from her eyes with her other hand.

"You can't leave the children, can you?" Michael said, trying to give her an honorable reason to stay.

She shook her head. "It would be irresponsible."

"It would," he said, fervently.

Just then, the heavens opened. The big, heavy raindrops that had been threatening all morning fell on the drive, on the suitcase, on Michael and on the polished wooden arms of the chair.

Yet Katie didn't even seem to notice that it was raining. "But all this between us makes it impossible."

For a moment, it looked as if she were about to pick up the bloody suitcase and take to the road again. So Michael forced himself to lie. "It was only a kiss, Katie. It was nothing. We can pretend it didn't happen, if you like," " he said. He was pleased that his voice sounded reasonable, rational even.

"Can we?" she said.

"Yes," he said, with easy confidence, hoping she'd believe him. "Good heavens, Katie, do you think I haven't kissed the help before?"

He hadn't, as it happened. There had been plenty of spoiled, rich girls at tennis parties, of course, and horsy young women from good county families, and then his fiancée, Connie. He'd never been remotely interested in a servant until he saw Katie, but this was not the moment to take her into his confidence.

She scowled at him, but he remained calm, biding his time as his clothes soaked to his skin in the downpour.

"Katie, the war makes us behave a little oddly at times. You and I have been thrown together, and it's awkward. But the war will be over soon and you'll go off and meet some chap and . . . "

"Don't! I don't like thinking of the future."

"Then think about today. Think about your duty here, your war work." God, Michael thought to himself, he was beginning to sound just like Marjory Mallory.

Katie glanced at him, with a guilty, sheepish look. "I suppose it would be wrong to walk out and leave the children to get used to someone new," she said at last.

Michael smiled. "Yes. Now, pick up that suitcase, before it goes soggy. I bet it's one of those awful cardboard ones, isn't it?"

"Probably," she said. "I've never given it a thought."

"Most inferior," he replied.

Then he cursed himself for being tactless with her yet again. Fine sets of leather suitcases were undoubtedly beyond Katie Rafferty's experience. "Let's talk it all over back at the house."

*Darling.* He would have liked to have added that word but it was more pragmatic not to. He must ease her in gently, like a nervous young mare. "I'll carry the suitcase, if you like."

She laid it across his knees to keep his hands free to wheel the chair. He shook it and almost laughed.

"It's a bit light, Katie. Were you in such a hurry to escape me that you forgot to pack?"

"Maybe," she admitted.

*

The house felt chilly to the two of them in their wet clothes, and he asked Katie to strike a match and light the fire that was laid in the grate. She knew well how to coax a fire into life, breathing on it to help the kindling take, then holding a sheet of newspaper over the grate to draw the flames. After a few moments, the fire began to take a hold and give out the first signs of warmth.

"It'll soon warm up," she said, as she took off her wet jacket and rubbed her hands in front of the gathering warmth of the logs burning in the grate. "Let me take your jacket, sir, and hang it by the fire. I'll fetch you another one. We don't want you catching a chill."

"You're worried about me, Katie, and that's very sweet."

"You wouldn't have got soaking wet in the first place, if you hadn't been running after me."

He smiled. "I *ran* after you?" he said, and raised an eyebrow.

"In a manner of speaking, sir."

He said nothing, but reflected upon the fact that she could have outrun him, had she been determined to. He felt a little surge of happiness and excitement, because there was only one conclusion to be made.

She wanted to be caught.

# Chapter Eleven

Katie approached the village hall on Arthur Perkins' arm. The music was already blaring into the street. The girl taking the money at the door held the blackout curtain out of the way, and they went inside.

"This is very jolly, isn't it?" Arthur seemed extremely pleased with himself.

"Yes!" Katie gazed up at the crepe paper streamers, all fanning out from a central point in the middle of the ceiling.

"Shall I fetch you a drink?"

Katie nodded and hoped desperately that Arthur wasn't getting the wrong idea. Perhaps it would have been better to have rejected all the invitations. But she couldn't help being a little curious about the last and the liveliest part of the May Day celebrations in Market Farrenden. It was world famous, if you believed the locals.

France may have fallen, and the Allies ousted from Dunkirk, but Hitler wasn't going to stop the village dance. Now that she was here, Katie was glad. The convivial atmosphere lifted the weight of responsibility from her shoulders. The hall was rather brightly lit and lots of people, young and old alike, chatted animatedly getting into the spirit of the evening. Some of the keenest dancers were already trying out their best moves.

Arthur headed for the corner where punch was served, weaving through the crowd greeting people as he went. And over on the far side, closely guarded by Mrs. Mallory and other stalwarts from the Women's Institute, was a long table covered with a red checkered cloth. Those refreshments—the big draw for some of the people here—would be savored later.

Katie scarcely had time to sip her drink when Arthur begged her for a dance. And she was amazed to find that when she wasn't dancing with Arthur, she was in hot demand with the other villagers, too. There was Harry Hammond, of course, who offended his own date to haul Katie into an energetic rumba. One by one, the butcher's boy, the bank clerk with the bad leg and several young men in uniform approached her. Katie danced all night, and when she wasn't dancing, she had to accept the drinks they offered, just to get a chance to catch her breath.

*

Michael waited for her in the darkness, idly running the wheelchair across the marble tiles in the hall. He stopped when he thought heard her footsteps, but it was a false alarm.

He fumed, thinking of the reasons why she was out so late, cursing himself for not taking her to the dance himself. He couldn't think of a worse punishment than watching her forming an attachment to some oaf from the village.

Finally he heard her light step on the stone terrace. He wheeled himself backwards a few inches and lurked in the shadows until she came indoors. He saw her skirts swirl as she closed the door. He heard her high-heeled shoes clattering across the floor, the very sound of a happy, carefree woman.

"Did you have a pleasant evening?"

She gave a gasp of surprise. "You gave me a start, sir!"

Michael rolled out of the shadows, and looked up at her. "I was just asking about the dance."

"It was fun, yes."

She looked lovely, he thought as he admired her curvaceous little figure and her red, red lips. She must have been the belle of the ball. "Did Hammond drop you off?"

"No, I wasn't risking a drive at night with him," she said, with a slightly tipsy laugh. "Heaven knows where I would have ended up."

"So who dropped you off? I heard a car. I thought you went

with Constable Perkins, and he's only got a bicycle."

"You are very well informed about my social arrangements, I see." Katie's tone was colder now.

It was none of his business, Michael knew that, but he was determined to get it out of her. "Who dropped you off?"

"If you must know, it was Marjory Mallory. She borrowed the van from the grocer and took it upon herself to take nine of us home. I was the last one, since I live all the way out here with you."

There was a long pause while Michael digested this information.

"Does that satisfy you?"

"I suppose so." He said, fuming inwardly. What right did she have to talk to him about satisfaction? "Did you dance with lots of men, Katie?"

"No, not really. Many of them are away at the war. Apparently there were lots of wallflowers."

"I don't believe you were one of them," he said, in what he knew was an acid tone of voice. "Did you kiss anyone?"

"Sir! You said that what happened between us was nothing, and that I was free to do as I pleased."

"God, you did! Who was he? Surely it wasn't Perkins?"

"The only kiss I got tonight was a peck on the cheek from the vicar," she insisted. But when he studied her, a flush colored her cheeks—he could see it even across the gloom in this room.

"I'm not sure I believe you, Katie."

She sighed, and gave a short impatient glance upwards. "If you wanted to keep an eye on me, sir, why didn't you come to the dance?"

"I hate dance music. You know that."

"You listened to it here, with me and the children, just the other day."

He paused, knowing what he wanted to say, knowing it was unwise. He gave in to the temptation all the same. "Would you have gone to the dance with me, if I'd asked you, Katie?"

"I wouldn't have had much choice."

It was not the answer he wanted to hear. He gave a huff of despair and released the brakes on the chair. He made it pivot smartly, and turned away from her. He wheeled himself away down the corridor, moving swiftly along to his rooms, hoping she wouldn't follow.

If she did, she would see him in tears.

# Chapter Twelve

"Katie. I have an appointment in London on Friday," Michael announced when their paths crossed by chance outside the library. "I'm seeing another surgeon about my back."

Good, Katie thought. A breathing space from the angst. The kiddies might calm down at least. "I hope it goes well, sir."

"Thank you. I need you to come with me."

Katie was certain she must have misheard.

"It's just for a couple of days. I've booked us into the Savoy."

"The Savoy Hotel?" she said, in astonishment.

"Yes, I always go there."

"You want *me* to go to the Savoy Hotel with you?"

"That's about the size of it. Can you make the necessary arrangements with Jessop?"

"Sir, is this some kind of joke—some schoolboy prank I am not familiar with?"

"No. I need you to come to London with me on Friday."

She could see he was starting to get annoyed. Katie shook her head. "It's impossible, sir. I need to stay here with the children."

It must have been the look on her face just before she shook her head that really angered him. His grip tightened on the polished wooden arms of the wheelchair. "There was a time," he said, through barred teeth, "when any girl I asked would have been *thrilled* to go to London with me."

Katie looked up at him, feeling more disgusted than ever before. "Even if she were one of your servants?" she asked.

"*Especially* if she was one of my servants."

Katie shook her head. "I can't agree to it, sir."

"As your employer, I could insist that you obey me."

"You could, sir," she said, "but that would be unreasonable. It would be most improper for us to go to London and stay the night there. What will people think?"

"May I remind you that they will *not* think you are having a torrid affair with a man in a wheelchair!" he yelled.

"Michael, you engaged me to look after the boys. Someone has to get them up and ready for school, somebody has to—"

"I've approached Marjory Mallory, and she's willing to come up on Thursday night and stay until Saturday afternoon, when we return."

He had it all worked out.

"Why don't you ask Mrs. Mallory to go with you to London, then, if she's so ready to help?"

"Because I would much prefer to go with you. I don't want Marjory bossing me about as if she was taking me to prep school for the first time!"

He had a point. That's exactly how Mrs. Mallory would treat him. But it was still highly irregular and would cause no end of gossip in the village. "I don't want to be the foolish girl that everyone is laughing about, sir."

"Katie," he pleaded. "I'm sorry. It was offensive, what I said before about taking girls up to London. I don't know why I imagined making you think I'm a cad would help."

"I can assure you it hasn't."

"I've got to see a new fellow, a specialist. He runs a private clinic in Harley Street. He's my last hope as far as getting out of this thing goes. My very last hope."

She bit her lip.

"Please, Katie. I'm . . . I'm nervous."

He had to force that last word out.

"You're nervous?" she said, with just a hint of skepticism.

"Very. It would help if I had someone with me, especially if it isn't good news. Someone who will help me discuss the doctor's advice."

"That might be rather a lot to expect from an ignorant Irish nursemaid."

"Katie, you are not that."

"Irish? I can assure you that I am," she said. "I'm pretty sure I'm a nursemaid, too, and unless the terms of my employment have changed, trips to Harley Street were not included . . . "

"Ignorant. You are not ignorant."

Katie went upstairs to pack. She was going to London, with a man—her employer, no less. The stationmaster would tell his wife, and she would tell her sister, who ran the post office and she would tell the entire village.

Katie looked through her meager collection of clothing. She had a smart navy blue hat, because hats were not on ration. That was a start. She tried it on and admired herself in the mirror. It set off her auburn curls to perfection, and with scarlet lipstick and fake pearls, she'd look presentable, but only from the neck up. It was what to wear below that bothered her. Her serge skirt was perhaps the next smartest thing she possessed, but it had seen a lot of wear and had been patched and darned. She had a gray blouse and a cardigan that she had knitted herself out of darning wool. It made a shabby ensemble. She imagined herself going through the door of the Savoy Hotel and sighed.

"It isn't important how I look," she murmured, "it's what I do for people that counts. Michael sacrificed his health for his country, and he needs me. Supporting him is the right thing to do."

"You're talking to yourself again, Miss Rafferty."

Katie gave a start, and swung round to find Roy standing in the doorway with Bob beside him. The smaller boy came in, uninvited, and knelt shyly on the bed, fingering the shiny buttons on Katie's clothing.

Bob had a surprising interest in ladies apparel, Katie had noticed.

"What are you going to wear at night?" he wanted to know.

"This," said Katie, and stuffed her long, shapeless blue nightie into the bag. Bob immediately got it out again and examined it critically.

Roy sniffed. "Not very alluring, is it?"

Katie was surprised Roy even knew the word.

"And what would you know about being 'alluring,' Roy?"

"More than you'd think. Me mum was a working girl."

"What did you say?"

"A tart. A one-woman knocking shop."

"Roy! Don't speak about your late mother like that! I'm sure she was no such thing. She'd probably be mortified to know you'd even uttered those words."

Roy sniffed again. "She'd have gone for shocking pink. Or black, with lots of lace and not much material."

"Yes, yes, well I don't possess anything along those lines, Roy, so I'll be taking my ordinary nightie, thank you very much. It's not as if I need to impress anyone. I'm not packing my trousseau." And most likely, she never would, Katie thought to herself. She hadn't exactly succeeded in saving herself for a white wedding.

"He's got a crush on you, anyone can see that. That's why he wants you to go with him."

"He has to have someone go with him, Roy, he can't manage otherwise."

"He didn't ask Mrs. Jessop, the crumbly old hatchet face. And he's taking you to the bleedin' Savoy, for goodness sake. There's only ever one reason why a toff takes a girl like you to the Savoy. Grow up, Katie."

Katie was scandalized that she was receiving these home truths from a twelve-year-old boy. She reddened with horrified embarrassment. "Will you shut your mouth before I ask you to wash it out with soap and water?"

Then she realized that Bob was trying to put on the blue nightie, and had almost gotten lost inside it.

"Don't do that, Bob, there's a dear, you might put your foot through it," Katie declared. "And then what will I do?"

"You'll have to sleep in the altogether," Roy said with a snigger.

"Roy, I am going to slap your face in a minute. Bob, give me that right now." She reached out and wrestled the blue nightie away from the child and flung it down into the depths of her overnight bag.

"Out, the pair of you!"

Reluctantly, the smaller boy scuttled out of the room and Roy sauntered off.

Katie was left to ponder two important questions. Had Roy's late mother really been a "one-woman knocking shop," and was he right about his lordship's intentions?

# Chapter Thirteen

Katie grabbed her hat and coat and picked up her bag from where it was sitting on the concrete bed. She checked her makeup in the tiny mirror and hurried downstairs to the front hall, where Michael was waiting for her. Her heart almost died when she saw him.

"Why are you dressed like that?" she said, in alarm.

It was six o'clock in the morning. He was wearing his RAF uniform—the whole outfit, including the peaked cap. The dress uniform of a flying officer. It was air force blue, like his eyes, and it suited him.

"I'm perfectly entitled to wear it," he said tersely. "I'm still in the RAF."

She tried to slow her breathing down to normal. She was anxious enough about this trip to London, without this. It probably was the same jacket. The one he had worn that night in the Tube station. She could remember the rough texture of the wool against her face. She remembered him calling her a brave girl. And then the pain and the heartache that came after.

"Technically, I'm still on sick leave," he explained.

"Sick leave?"

"Yes. I've come up for review a few times, and I keep putting them off."

"Why, for heaven's sake? They'll have to discharge you in the end."

"Not if I get better first."

*But you aren't going to get better.* She stopped herself just in time from saying it aloud.

Hammond arrived to take them to the station. It was a cold, crisp morning and Katie shivered as they loaded Michael and the wheelchair into the old black Austin. She tucked a plaid blanket over his knees.

"Don't," Michael grumbled. "I feel like some decrepit relic from the Boer Wars when you do things like that."

"I don't want you catching a chill."

Perhaps it was too late. His manner was very chilly indeed.

*

Michael picked at the plaid blanket that lay over his knees and fumed. For years he had caught trains at this platform—trains that took him away to boarding school or to the seaside during the holidays. Trains to Cambridge University where he was a madcap student with all his friends. Trains to London to see shows, and to flying school, and away to the war.

Never before had he caught a train looking and feeling like this.

"Bloody train will be late, of course."

Katie smiled weakly at him. "It isn't even ten to, yet, sir. If it came now it would be early."

He ignored her and made a few more gloomy predictions about how long they might have to wait. "These days the trains don't run according to the timetable at all. I think it's a deliberate strategy to confuse the enemy—and it will, if the invasion ever comes."

"God willing, it won't," Katie said. "You RAF boys have seen to that."

Michael was rather gratified to hear her talk about him like that. RAF boys. That was the world he knew. That was where he belonged. Miraculously, the train steamed into the station only seven minutes after it was due.

Michael bore the indignity of being carried onto the train in the porter's arms as stoically as he could, and finally they were on board, in a compartment all to themselves.

Michael arranged his useless legs in front of him so they looked like the legs of any languid young man. His smartly pressed RAF trousers were loose enough to hide the wasted muscles, and his black leather shoes had been polished to a high shine.

Katie was sitting beside him, wearing brown hand-knitted gloves—awful things some elderly aunt in Ireland must have given to her for Christmas, he supposed, and Katie was much too thrifty to throw them away. He'd love to get her some new clothes, but that was complicated, what with the shortages. He supposed he'd have to get her something on the black market. He'd like to get her out of those clothes, though. Then he smiled. Yes, he'd *love* to get her out of those clothes.

She seemed determined to engage him in conversation, although he would have been quite content to gaze out of the window and watch the melancholy English countryside slip by. But she was a chatty little thing. Michael tried to resist her conversational gambits at first, giving only clipped, defensive replies. Katie, quite clearly, had other ideas.

"Why does Mrs. Mallory owe you a favor?" she asked.

"It's a long story."

"Tell it to me."

He sighed before smiling. Resistance was useless.

"Marjory's son Peter was a flyer, like me," he began. "We trained together, with several other friends of mine, from school."

"She leaned forward expectantly, and he could see from the way her eyes sparked with interest that she was hoping for a good yarn. He'd do his best.

"We were great chums . . . "

"Oh, I love the way you say *chums*! I've never heard anyone say that before."

Michael scowled. "Don't keep interrupting. We were the best of friends. But Peter was in a couple of nasty dogfights—one of them badly damaged his plane and he limped back to the aerodrome with the wings full of holes and smoke pouring out. He belly flopped on the runway. All the emergency vehicles had to scoot over and put him out. Peter climbed out of the hatch without a scratch on him, but his nerves were shot to pieces. Usually we laughed off such things in the officers' mess and we were fine next time we had to go up. But not Peter. He said if he got back into that cockpit one more time, he was a dead man. He convinced himself he'd die if he flew again, because his number had been up that time and yet somehow he had managed to bring his plane in. His whole attitude changed, and people started calling him a coward."

"Is that the reason Mrs. Mallory is so keen to do her patriotic duty, because of Peter?" Katie interjected.

"Marjory has patriotism like the rest of us have sandbags, Katie. Peter was tremendously patriotic, too, at the start of the war. But the near miss broke him. Of course, that kind of attitude didn't go down too well and the RAF was desperately short of good pilots. The medical officer said he was fit, and I knew if I didn't step in, Peter would be hauled up in front of a disciplinary committee. I pulled some strings for him. I got him sent to a different MO, who wrote up a report about Peter's nerves. Then I called up a fellow I knew from my Cambridge days and got Peter assigned to a desk job. Peter didn't feel good about it. In fact, he hated himself, but he accepted the job. I have to say, flying a desk suits him, and he's still alive. He's the only one left out of the whole gang of us apart from me. And I hardly qualify as being alive, do I?"

"Don't be ridiculous. Of course you're alive."

"Alive, but not *kicking*, Katie. Not unless these doctors can sort me out."

Yet today, he did feel alive—the train was steaming through the countryside and he was sitting beside a very pretty girl.

Since the wheelchair was in the guard's van, people passing up and down the corridor might not even notice that he was disabled. He felt a little surge of satisfaction at the thought. The waiter brought them some coffee and offered him the morning paper, which Michael accepted, though he didn't even bother to glance at it. He was too busy enjoying sitting next to Katie, chatting brightly to her, seeing her smile back at him, while the soft gray-green English countryside slipped by and they rolled closer and closer to London.

*

Katie swallowed hard when the train pulled into the station. She hated London. It brought back too many memories. She adjusted her hat and checked her gloves, pulling them more firmly up to her wrists.

Michael seemed to sense her disquiet. He gave her hand a squeeze. "Don't worry, you'll be all right with me."

They had to wait until most people left the train, and then a brusque London porter helped them onto the platform.

"I've just realized something," Katie said. "We won't be taking the Tube, will we, sir?"

"Of course not. I couldn't possibly get down there, so we'll be taking a taxi instead."

"Good," she said. She had seen enough of London underground stations to last her a lifetime.

Michael was very quiet. She wondered if he, too, was remembering that time when he'd crossed the tracks and run lightly up the stairs two at a time. She still recalled how everyone on the crowded platform had stopped and stared at him—handsome, reckless young man that he was then.

Michael dictated the address and the taxi headed for Harley Street. The city was busy now, as people hurried to work before nine. The taxi passed a lot of bomb damage: new sites where people were still scavenging the wreckage for anything salvageable, and old sites where the weeds had started to grow. The driver took a circuitous route saying that some streets were impassable. It might have been true, but Katie suspected he wanted to bump up the fare. It was an odd feeling, knowing that Michael had enough money not to care about things like that.

The doctor's was not like any Katie had seen. There were no

hordes of people, hacking and coughing, queuing up to see the doctor. There were no harassed Irish mammies with children clutching at their skirts and sickly babies in their arms. There were no injured laborers nursing a nasty cut they acquired on a building site. Instead, they were ushered into a plush lobby beautifully furnished with mahogany furniture and thick deep carpets. A receptionist rose and greeted them with a crisp, cut-glass accent. They were shown in to the doctor's room right away.

A nurse wearing a starchy white headdress that looked like an enormous origami swan perched on top of her head preceded the doctor. She helped Michael undress and took his blood pressure carefully. Katie was surprised how much she resented seeing another woman touching him so casually.

"I've already studied your old x-rays," the doctor explained as he entered, pondering the case with enormous dignity. "We'll do more today, of course, to see if anything has changed."

The specialist wanted to talk about the risks, but Michael only wanted to hear about the advantages and the marvelous improvements he might expect.

"I know you're keen," the doctor counseled, "but it would be unprofessional if I didn't advise you of the risks."

"Risks well worth taking, wouldn't you say?" Michael's face was eager and his eyes were so hopeful, Katie had to turn her gaze away.

"I'm sure you have dreams of walking again, perhaps even of flying, but I must warn you that there are limits to what we can reasonably expect from this procedure."

But Michael acted as if he didn't hear. He was all set to sign on the dotted line. "My mind is made up, doctor. How soon can you fit me in?"

Katie knew she had to intervene. "Michael, you asked me to come along and listen, and the doctor seems to be saying this might not be such a good idea."

Michael frowned and she stopped speaking, not wanting to

hurt his feelings. He had such a youthful, optimistic look on his face. She'd never seen him looking so elated, as if life were full of possibilities. Perhaps the only time she'd seen him looking anything like this was that day she gave him the ill-considered kiss.

"You must think about the complications, Michael. It would be very disappointing if you went through this surgery and ended up worse," the doctor chimed in. "It's a big decision. You must talk things over with your lovely wife. Take your time, and let me know if you want to proceed when you have thought it all over properly."

Katie froze, awkward that the doctor misunderstood her role. She waited for Michael to correct him but he didn't. He did blush, though.

The doctor leaned forward and spoke again. "Is that a motivation for having this operation, Michael—to enable you to make love to your wife as before?"

Katie blushed too and bit her lip, but she kept quiet. This was Michael's show to run.

Michael stammered his reply. "Every man wants to . . . " His voice cracked.

This must be awful for him, Katie thought. No wonder he hadn't wanted to face this alone. Rashly, she took his hand and squeezed it to give him courage, though she knew it would continue to send the doctor the wrong message. The doctor smiled at them, sympathetically.

"I would hope that, as a couple, you are exploring your sexuality to the full. Enjoying each other, giving each other pleasure, finding out what you can do, rather than worrying too much about what you can't."

Katie knew her face must be scarlet now. She swallowed and prayed for fortitude. She glanced at Michael, who was staring angrily at his useless legs, unable to meet the doctor's gaze. It was as if he had gone into a private world of his own, where all he could think about was how to get well.

In direct answer to prayer, the nurse with the extraordinary headdress returned to inform the doctor that his next appointment had just arrived. Katie heaved an audible sigh of relief. Michael came out of his trance, too.

"Thank you so much for explaining it all to me," he said. "I shall read all the literature you've given me and inform you of my decision in a day or two."

In the taxi, Katie tried to reach out and take his hand again, expecting he would need sympathy. Instead, he was wildly optimistic about the surgery.

"Did you hear him? He spoke about me walking again, Katie, flying again."

It was as if Michael hadn't been in the same room as her.

"He spoke about risks and dangers. He didn't say any of those things were possible."

"Of course they're possible, Katie! I've read about cases like mine, people who made a complete recovery."

"I know," she said. "But the doctor said that there's no guarantee. You must have heard him say that?"

"That's just medical waffle. This surgery is cutting-edge medicine. That's why I want it so much. It will change my life. It will change our lives, Katie."

There it was again. *Our lives?*

Katie sighed. And yet, she couldn't ask him why he had let the doctor think they were husband and wife. She dared not return to that hideous moment during the consultation. But she didn't want to hurt him, either. His hopes and dreams would be dashed soon enough, unless she could think of a way to talk him out of it.

# Chapter Fourteen

The Savoy's luxurious dining room overlooked the Thames, and tonight there was a band playing jolly dance music with the promise of a vocalist later. The tables were arranged around the edge of a lovely polished dance floor.

Katie got Michael settled and found him a napkin.

"I can manage that perfectly well myself. I'm twenty-six, you know, not eighty-nine."

She ignored him and laid the napkin carefully over his lap. He scowled at her in protest, which reminded her of Roy. She took her seat opposite him. The tables were small and intimate for a restaurant this grand. Katie studied the menu and noticed that the prices weren't listed. She assumed Michael had been here before as he seemed perfectly at ease and not remotely concerned about the cost. He wouldn't even look at the menu until he'd ordered a bottle of champagne. The waiter scurried off and fetched it straight away.

The food was described in French, which Michael translated for her, putting on the most appalling French accent and adding a lot of "*oui, oui, oui*" noises to make her laugh.

Only then did she reveal she'd learned French at the convent school where she attended and was perfectly capable of recognizing a "*pomme de terre*" when she saw one.

"Forgive me, mademoiselle, for doubting any part of your education. I'm sure the nuns taught you everything a young woman needs to know!"

"Well, not quite everything, no," she admitted ruefully. "There were some things we had to find out for ourselves!"

They both laughed at that.

They ate their starters and drank their champagne, and Katie began to feel merry and light-headed. It was lovely, sitting here like this, with a handsome young man. The main course was divine—she wouldn't have thought it possible to get food like that in wartime.

The music was louder now, and she had to lean forward to hear what Michael was saying. He leaned forward attentively, too, and his fingers kept playing with the stem of her glass. He told a joke he knew about drinking champagne, and she heard her own laughter bubbling over as if someone had popped a cork inside her.

But now his fingers were no longer touching the stem of her glass; they were stroking hers instead, and all the time he was talking animatedly as if he didn't know what he was doing. Except that she was sure he did. And the more she let him get away with, the more he did, and the more she realized that she liked it.

A warm flush of desire rose inside her. Never in a million years would she have expected to have dinner with a man like this. The war had a lot to answer for, and a few things to thank.

When the other patrons began to dance, Katie turned to watch. One girl in particular whirled around in a lovely dress, tight in the arms of a man in an RAF uniform. Katie wondered how on earth she could have spared the coupons for this latest fashion, now that rationing was in force. She snuck a peek at Michael, who was watching the couple with a longing, wistful look on his face.

"I wish I could dance with you," he said, and those few words said it all.

Katie squeezed his hand. "But if we were dancing, we couldn't do this," she said. She scooched over to place the lightest, gentlest kiss on his cheek.

The flicker of surprise was soon replaced by a teasing grin. "That's not fair. You told me that was off limits."

She was so thankful she had made him smile again. "Blame the champagne," she quipped.

"Waiter!" Michael called out, in a loud, theatrical tone, "I shall require another bottle!"

Katie laughed and shook her head at his play-acting. But then his face went rather serious and he leaned in toward her.

"Do you want a proper kiss?" he asked softly.

Her heart skittered inside her as he touched her chin and tilted it toward him. She waited, expecting him to kiss her straight away, but instead he hesitated, achingly close. He smiled and his lashes almost brushed against her face.

"You're teasing me," she murmured quietly.

"Yes, I am," he whispered, and she could feel the warmth of his breath on her cheek. He stroked the side of her face, just once, and made her shiver with longing. "You're very sweet."

"Please," she whispered. She wished he would either kiss her or put an end to her suffering.

"Are you asking me to kiss you?" he said.

"Yes."

So he did. He let his lips meet hers expertly and then he kissed her like a movie star—tenderness, experience, passion—all in one lasting kiss. He didn't seem to care that they were in a restaurant, with people around. Instead, he let the sensation build and build, until there was more passion, more ardor, and more eroticism in this kiss than she had ever experienced before.

She was almost gasping with a mixture of desire and shock when he drew away. He had made her feel like she was on the silver screen, too; she had felt glamorous and confident in the throes of the moment. When it had ended, she found she felt like a silly, inexperienced convent girl again.

Her heart was pounding, the champagne making her dizzy, clouding her judgment. She couldn't give in to these feelings, and yet, she just had. She had indulged in that sensational kiss with Michael. She glanced about the room but nobody seemed especially interested in her moral dilemma. She gazed back into Michael's eyes as if hoping to find the answer there, but he just smiled and followed with more kisses. Insanity had taken hold of her body and soul the moment she let him put his warm lips on hers, the instant she let him slide his wicked silver tongue into her mouth.

She pushed him away. He was a naughty man, she decided. Sitting there cool as you please making her think the most sinful thoughts she'd ever had in her life. "Did you book two rooms?" she blurted out, desperately.

"Of course," he said, giving her a very direct glance. "But they are adjoining."

Her hands went up to her scarlet face. "I couldn't, sir! You don't expect me to, do you?"

"Would you like to?"

"No!"

He smiled. "Are you sure? The doctor suggested we try."

"The doctor thought we were married. If you brought me here thinking that I'm fair game, you're in for a disappointment, sir. There are some mistakes that I will *not* make again!"

"You thought about it, though, just for a moment," he reflected, with a hint of satisfaction in his voice.

"I'm not that kind of girl, Michael."

He scowled. He leaned back in the wheelchair, picking at the armrest in a discontented sort of way. "I wish we could have danced," he said, the regret coming back into his voice. "It might have helped to put you at ease."

"I doubt that very much," said Katie.

"Shall we ask them what's for pudding?" he said, anxious to dispel both the sadness and the embarrassment stealing the shine from the interlude.

She nodded.

He raised his hand to signal for the dessert trolley. After a few moments, a very elegant woman began to make her way to their table, but the cakes and pies were nowhere to be seen.

"Oh my God," Michael said.

This approaching woman was definitely *not* a member of the hotel staff. She wore a figure-hugging, jet black evening gown that shimmered as she walked. And then Katie realized she, too, recognized the face.

"Michael, darling," the woman said, as she planted a kiss on Michael's cheek. "And in uniform too! I *am* surprised."

"Connie." His tone was cold.

"You were Michael's fiancée," Katie stated, and then she cringed. The champagne must have loosened her foolish, foolish tongue.

"I was." Connie replied in a cool tone. "Michael, who is this charming young person?"

"This is Katie, she's my . . . " he obviously didn't want to say housekeeper. Katie wasn't even sure what her official title was in Michael's mind.

"Sweetheart," Katie plunged in rashly.

Michael gave her the warmest look of wonder and admiration she had ever seen. He took Katie's hand and gave it a grateful squeeze.

He turned back to Connie, and his expression hardened. "Forgive me if I don't get up, Connie."

"Of course. Poor darling. It must be so frustrating."

"I was sorry to hear about Reg," Michael said.

"Yes, it was very tragic." Connie said. "I'm a widow at twenty-three."

"And still in mourning, I see."

Connie glanced down at the clingy black gown she was wearing. "One has to carry on, Michael."

"One carries on with most of the squadron, by the look of it." Michael glanced back at the table that Connie had just left. A long table full of laughing young men, with one or two girlfriends scattered among them like stray petunias in a bed of ageratum. She gave one of the men a flirtatious little wave.

"If I'd known you would be churlish," she said. "I wouldn't have bothered to say hello."

"Perhaps that would have been for the best."

"I forgot to ask what brings you to London, Michael?"

"I'm here to visit my surgeon. He thinks he can mend my back."

"Really?" A spark of real interest flickered behind Connie's pale gray eyes. "How extraordinary. The doctors seemed to think there was so little hope."

"You thought there was *no* hope, Connie."

Her face hardened. "I must join my friends before I'm missed. Goodnight, Michael. It's been such a pleasure!"

"Goodbye, Connie."

When she was gone, Michael let out a long, bitter sigh. "That's the trouble with the Savoy," he said. "You run into people from the past."

Katie bit her lip. "She was a bit unpleasant."

"We all make mistakes, Katie."

She couldn't argue with that.

\*

I don't have to make any mistakes with him tonight, Katie promised herself as she pushed Michael along the corridor. *I'm older and wiser, and he is my employer. I don't have to do anything I don't want to do.*

She pushed him into the lift and pressed the button. It creaked into life, carrying them slowly to the floor above.

"The Savoy was one of the first hotels with an electric lift," Michael told her. "Which is lucky, isn't it?"

She smiled, though she was standing behind him and he didn't see. "They must have seen you coming, sir."

"Katie, thank you for today."

"You don't need to thank me. It was no hardship and you've made the whole trip so nice for me, sir. Taxis and that wonderful meal."

The doors opened and they rolled along the plushy carpeted corridor to find their rooms.

"I need you to help me undress," he said.

"I know."

She checked the number on the key, and found the right door.

"I could do it myself, normally, it's just that in an unfamiliar place . . . "

"It's perfectly all right, sir."

"I do wish you'd stop calling me 'sir.'"

"It's a habit. It would be difficult to break now. Sir."

She steered him into the room, hoping to take her mind off how nervous she felt being alone with him. She parked the chair beside the bed and he made an agile maneuver from one to the other. He eased himself back onto the pillows before switching on the bedside lamp and illuminating the room with a warm, golden light.

She bustled about, unpacking his things and laying them in convenient places he could reach. She picked up the book he was reading— yet another book about recovering from a back injury.

"Do you want me to leave this on the right side of the bed or the left?"

"Katie, stop fussing and help me get undressed."

It was time to stop delaying and get on with it. She eased him out of his RAF jacket, trying to ignore the longing that welled up in her. It seemed that the more clothes he took off, the stronger and more confused her emotions became. She'd never felt such a yearning for a man before—not for Tom, not for anyone. She undid his shirt buttons for him, one by one by one, revealing the glorious contours of his chest.

Suddenly she looked up at him, abashed. "You could have done that yourself."

He smiled. "Yes," he said, softly, "but I would much rather you did it for me."

She slipped the shirt off his shoulders and breathed in deeply. She loved the look of his upper body—all the curved muscles beautifully defined in the golden light from the lamp. Michael's skin was pale, like a marble statue, and she could hardly take her eyes off him.

He reached out and touched her face, a gentle caress, full of promise and pleasures yet to come. "Would you like me to kiss you some more?"

"No! No, I wouldn't. Absolutely not."

*

The lady protests too much, Michael thought to himself. He remembered saying those words, to another pretty girl, long ago. He didn't say them to Katie. With her, he felt like a tongue-tied, nervous schoolboy.

He wasn't sure what to say, or what to do next. If he hadn't been injured, he would have seduced her, expertly, and the early stages would have been skillful and swift. He would have struck while she was still dizzy from the champagne. While they were dancing, he would have whispered in her ear about the spectacular view of the Thames from his bedroom window. She would have giggled and protested, but he would have pulled her along by the hand and kissed and cuddled her all the way up in the lift.

It would have been him, not her, who slipped the key into the lock and pulled her into the room. Then, pushing her slim body back against the door to close it, he would have kissed her fiercely—aggressively almost—until she melted against him. He wouldn't even have bothered to turn on the light, and before long, she'd have been ready to slide down onto the floor with him in a weakened state of passion and longing.

Instead, he would have carried her to the bed, and she wouldn't have done a damn thing about it. Oh, she would have blushed and murmured when he took off her clothes, but she would have let him undress her all the same. Stepping away from the bed for a moment, his own clothes would have been off in a few effortless moves while she enjoyed the striptease in the half-darkness. After that, he'd slow down the pace, kissing her here, and there, and everywhere until she begged him for it.

*Everything was different now.* He was sitting on the bed like a virgin recruit with the prettiest girl he'd ever seen, unable to decide what to do next. If he said or did the wrong thing, she be off like a frightened butterfly.

"Is that everything you need, sir?"

"Katie."

"I don't think I should be in here, sir, unless there's something important I've forgotten to do."

He didn't want her to go. He knew he had to do something and like a gauche young man on a first date, he clutched her hand.

It worked.

She sat down beside him on the bed. She let him fondle her hand in his, let him raise it to his lips and kiss it. Her soft brown eyes were patient, understanding, and vulnerable. He didn't quit while he was winning; he leaned in for a proper kiss. He put his mouth on hers and felt her trembling response. He encouraged her to put her arms around his neck and held her close against his bare chest. He was sure he could feel her quickening heartbeat, his own heart pounding madly, too. He tangled his hands in her glorious auburn hair, and kissed her hard. She made those sweet, sexy moans of enjoyment that women make when they are aroused.

"You like to kiss, don't you?"

"I like kissing you," she blurted.

"And I love kissing you," he murmured, with his lips against the warm, sensitive skin in the curve of her neck. He felt triumphant for a moment, and he pulled her down on to the bed beside him to lie in his arms. He experienced just a hint of the old self-confidence he used to feel with a woman. He knew that she wanted him, but his happiness in it was blighted. Blighted by his agonizing, aching fear that he couldn't give her what she wanted, even now she had admitted that she was enjoying this.

They lay side by side, in each other's arms, pretending they were just like any other couple, while Michael weighed the options.

There was no way he could make love to her, not like this.

He was half a man, and she was a whole, warm, wonderful woman. He could offer to pleasure her, perhaps, but that would mean admitting that he didn't think he could love her properly. He could achieve an erection, yes. He was luckier than some. But make love to her? Thrust inside her? Plant his seed deep within her body? Probably not. They could try, but it might be a disaster. He couldn't risk it. She deserved the finest lovemaking a man could give.

He could feel her breasts warm and heavy against him through the thin fabric of her blouse. That was an awful gray blouse she was wearing—he'd love to take it off, but he contented himself with holding her close. His left hand cupped the curve of her bottom. The texture of her blue serge skirt was all wrong-he wanted to feel her smooth, warm skin. He wanted to explore her, all of her.

*You can't keep leading her on like this, when you have nothing to give.*

"This is wrong, sir," she said, quietly.

"You think I don't know that?"

"Then why are you doing it?" she said. "Why are you tempting me like this?"

He was surprised. "Is that how you think of me? A temptation?"

"Yes."

He gave her a kiss on the forehead. "I'm grateful, even for that. I doubt that many women would give me a second glance, these days."

"Would you stop being so desperately sorry for yourself?"

"If I'm not allowed to feel sorry for myself, I don't know who is."

"But you are so lucky."

Michael gave an impatient sigh. "Lucky to be alive. It always comes down to that. Alive, yes, but able to have a life worth living? No."

She sat up, shocked. "You are very lucky in so many ways."

"It's torture for me to hold you in my arms and not be able to have you."

She stiffened. "I have no intention of letting you 'have me' as you so crudely put it, Michael. I am not that kind of girl."

He noticed that she had inadvertently called him Michael.

"Come on, Katie."

"I am not about to commit a mortal sin just because you bought me a first-class train ticket and a nice meal. I should never have lain down with you like this, but you wanted to kiss goodnight and that seemed harmless enough."

"If you stayed in my bed the whole bloody night, I doubt we could do anything that would amount to a mortal sin!"

"I must go," she quickly stood and straightened her skirt. "If I leave now, perhaps I shall save myself from hellfire and you won't have to face up to your feelings of inadequacy!"

"For heaven's sake, Katie, I want you to stay!"

"I have no intention of spending the night with you. I made that clear downstairs."

"I know what you said, Katie, but it wasn't what you meant. Just now, lying here together, you were ready for it."

"That is very bigheaded of you. Never presume to know a woman's thoughts, sir, because you can be gravely mistaken. Unlike every other floozy you may have known, I say what I mean and I mean what I say."

"And who are you to talk to me about floozies, Katie? You've got a history, too, haven't you!"

"If you are referring to that night in the underground station, you can stop right there. You don't know anything about me, and at this rate, you never will. I'm a decent girl. A night in the Savoy doesn't make me anybody's."

He was very offended. "I am not anybody."

"No, you are Lord High and Mighty Farrenden, my employer, which makes it even worse. Roy Luckens, a twelve-year-old boy, tried to warn me. I thought you had more integrity."

She flounced out of the room, slamming the door. There was a long empty silence, while Michael sat alone in the bed, stunned.

"That went well," he muttered out loud. He reached out and turned off the bedside lamp. Then he wrapped himself in the eiderdown and lay down, fuming with frustration inside.

*

The children seemed surprised Michael wasn't cured. Four little faces peered through the banisters on the great curved staircase, waiting to catch a first glimpse. Four little faces fell when they saw Katie pushing the wheelchair up the ramp into the house.

"It didn't work?" George said, in astonishment, as if he had expected to see Michael striding purposefully into the grand entrance hall on a pair of shiny new legs.

Katie explained the appointment was just a discussion about the possibility of an operation in the future, but apparently the nuances had been lost on them. She didn't dare tell them now that, in her opinion, Michael shouldn't commit himself to a lot of pain and agony with so little hope of an improvement.

"Aren't you going to do it, Mister Lord?" asked Alfie, all round-eyed curiosity.

"I don't want you to get your legs mended, Mister Lord," Bob announced, jutting his little chin out.

"Why not?" Michael wanted to know.

"Because I like having rides in the wheelchair."

"If it works and I don't need the chair any more, I'll give it to you for keeps. How about that?"

"I'm too small to do the wheels," Bob pointed out. "And I'd rather sit on your knee."

Everyone else took turns with their say, so Katie decided to have hers. "You don't have to go through with it," she said desperately, and her eyes scanned Michael's face. "You haven't signed anything yet and you're fine as you are.

"I'm not," he said, and his words were cold and crisp. Then he added in a cryptic whisper, "Things would have been different in London, if that were true."

Katie shook her head and glanced away. They were not going to discuss this in front of the children. "It could make things worse, not better."

"Why are you so dead set against this, Katie? I thought you were on my side."

Because I know it won't work, she thought, but she kept that to herself. "It's risky and very expensive."

"The cost is no concern of yours," Michael announced haughtily, "and I'm the one taking the risk."

# Chapter Fifteen

Michael was teaching the boys to play checkers on the scrubbed pine table and Katie was washing dishes the next Saturday afternoon when Mrs. Jessop appeared in the doorway. Michael frowned, resenting the interruption. "What is it, Lizzie?"

"There's a Private O'Brien calling."

Michael frowned. "Who?"

He didn't know anyone named O'Brien. Not on visiting terms, anyway. And most of his friends were in the RAF, not the Army.

"Some Irish boy in uniform, asking for Katie," Mrs. Jessop added, pursing her lips in disapproval.

Katie's knees instantly buckled, and she grabbed the edge of the sink to stay upright.

"He's in the library," said Mrs. Jessop, "and he looks like the sort of oaf who might break something valuable if we leave him alone in there for long."

"Oh dear God in heaven," Katie choked out, and Michael frowned. Katie wasn't prone to using blasphemy lightly.

"Is he your fancy man, then?" Roy inquired.

"Roy!" said Mrs. Jessop. "Just when we thought your manners were improving."

"I can't see him," Katie pleaded. "I can't."

That worried Michael. What had the man done that Katie was too scared to even look at him?

"Can we have a look at him?" Alfie asked, curiosity roused.

"Certainly not," Michael said. "He's Katie's visitor."

"I can't see him," she repeated, trembling in obvious fear.

Mrs. Jessop was getting impatient. "What do you want me to do with him, then? Send him away?"

"Could we do that?" Katie turned to appeal to Michael.

"Yes, we could," Michael said doubtfully, "but aren't you anxious to find out what he wants?"

Katie looked stricken.

"You think you know what he wants?" Michael asked, turning around in his chair to try to read Katie's face.

She turned from him and gazed out the window. She was breathing in a funny way, as if she couldn't get quite enough oxygen in her lungs.

"Can't we go and have a look at him, Mister Lord? Does he have red hair like Katie, Mrs. Jessop?"

Roy interjected. "He's not her bruvver. He's her boyfriend."

"No, he is not," Katie nearly screamed. She covered her face in her hands and to everyone's acute embarrassment, she started to cry. Michael knew he had to take charge of the situation before things devolved into any more chaos and confusion.

"I'll talk to him, Katie," Michael said, decisively.

"I'll have a few words with the man, wish him good luck in the war, and send him on his way."

"Good luck in the war!" Katie swung round sharply. "Mrs. Jessop? Are you *sure* he was in Army uniform?"

"Of course I'm sure. Private, First Class, British Army. His uniform is practically new. I'd say he's only recently enlisted."

"Oh dear God," Katie moaned. "Why would he do that?""

Alfie looked up. "Why don't you go and ask him?"

Katie just screwed up her apron in her hands and turned her head away.

Michael knew the mystery guest was Katie's former boyfriend and the father of her child, presumably. He wished he didn't have to face the man in this contraption. He reached the door, and hesitated for a moment. An idea came to him.

"Jessop, is the library door closed?"

"Yes, sir."

"Good. If you wheel me into my study, he won't see me go by.

Then if I get into an ordinary chair and sit at my desk, I'll look just like an ordinary bloke, won't I?"

"You never look like an *ordinary* bloke, Mister," Roy observed with a sniff.

"We can put the wheelchair out of sight, can't we?" Michael asked.

"Why can't he see the wheelchair?" Bob wanted to know.

"He wants more respect," Roy explained, toying with Katie's abandoned lunch on the table.

"Yes, Roy, I do. A little more from you might not go amiss, either. Jessop, find my RAF jacket. I think it's hanging in the hall."

Mrs. Jessop hurried into action, grasping the handles of the wheelchair and pushing Michael toward the door. "We'll get it on the way," she said, conspiratorially.

Safely ensconced in the study behind his rosewood desk, Michael arranged a few pieces of paperwork artistically in front of him. He nodded to show the man in.

The man who appeared in the doorway was tall and dark. Not as tall as he, Michael observed with a certain amount of satisfaction, and not as slender either. This man was broad-shouldered, built like a coal-heaver, with a rough-hewn look about him. But then, a lot of women liked that kind of thing, Michael thought ruefully. Katie had liked that kind of thing, once.

"Private O'Brien? Forgive me if I don't stand to greet you. I'm recovering from an injury, you understand."

"A war wound, sir?" O'Brien's eyes flickered with interest.

The impertinent fellow had an open face, with bright blue eyes. Dark brows above them, well-defined brow ridges—a strong, masculine countenance. Obviously Celtic.

"That's right. A dogfight. Didn't go so well for me. I bailed and came down on somebody's roof. Bit of a bumpy landing."

Michael often found the only way he could talk about what had been one of the worst events in his life was to play it down with a joke.

"Sounds like a real adventure, sir. A story to tell your grandchildren."

O'Brien gave a melodic Irish laugh and seemed genuinely impressed.

"Yes, yes, great fun." Michael tried to put the same twinkle into his own eyes although the mention of the grandchildren he was never likely to have was a little close to the bone. "Please, sit down."

O'Brien pulled up a chair. He was one of those men who couldn't sit neatly; he was all long, loose limbs and huge, hulking shoulders. Michael struggled to ignore mental images of Katie with this man— dancing with him, kissing him, and the rest. He tried to fight the images invading his mind: Katie in this man's powerful arms, her naked body against his. Oh God. Michael swallowed hard and forced himself to concentrate on the conversation at hand.

"How can I help you?" he said, and the words came out like bullets. Inwardly, Michael cursed, because he'd wanted to speak with that laconic air of disinterest people of his standing liked to use.

"Well, sir, it's Kathleen I've come to see. She works here, I understand?"

Michael had no idea her name was Kathleen; he'd assumed it was Catherine.

"My family is very friendly with hers back in Ireland," O'Brien added.

"Really? That's not the impression Katie has given me."

That was the first remark that seemed to unsettle O'Brien at all. He frowned, and his dark brows drew close together for a moment. "Look, I don't know what she's told you, but Katie and I were certainly very friendly for quite a while. And I need to see her. She's not answering my letters, you see, and I've got a number of things I need to ask her . . . "

"If she's not answering your letters," Michael said, leaning forward as if explaining basics to a foolish young cadet, "one might possibly draw the conclusion that Katie would rather leave the acquaintance in the past, where it belongs."

"She wouldn't do that. Not if she had a free choice. You don't know the full story. You don't know what she's like."

"Actually I've come to know Katie reasonably well over the last few months. I've grown rather fond of her, in fact. And I know more about Katie's past than you might expect."

O'Brien blanched. He turned his dark green cap round and round in his hands, thinking what to say next. "So that's the way of it, is it?"

"I'm afraid it is."

O'Brien sighed sharply and got to his feet. "Have you even told her I'm here?"

"I have. She didn't want to speak with you." Michael felt that he had to add something to convince the man so he kept talking. "She seemed very surprised you had enlisted in the British Army."

O'Brien's face darkened, and Michael knew he had been right to throw in that little detail. It obviously struck a chord with the man.

"She was in love with me!" O'Brien protested. "Far more in love with me than I was with her—at that time at least. I won't believe she's finished with me until I've heard it from her own mouth."

"People's feelings change. Especially when they've been treated shabbily."

O'Brien's face flashed with anger. "Who are you to talk about treating people shabbily—sitting there behind your fancy desk telling me lies about my Katie? I'm leaving for the frontline soon and I need to see her. If you really know what happened between us, you'll understand why. But perhaps you're just bluffing. Tell her I'm on my last pass, and I must talk to her before I go. Tell her I've got a room at the pub in the village and I'm staying until tomorrow."

Michael realized he was shaking with rage and hoped desperately it didn't look like fear. The adrenalin coursed through his veins and he wanted with all his heart to jump up and grab the man by the lapels of that brand new jacket. He needed to shake some sense into him after the condition he'd left Katie in, the filthy swine. Perhaps it was just as well he was unable to get up, lest he laid the man out cold on the Axminster carpet.

Mrs. Jessop had already come to the door, startled by the sound of raised voices. She looked questioningly at Michael, waiting for his instructions.

Michael managed to gather his wits about him. "I think it is high time we terminated our discussion. Jessop, show Private O'Brien the way out, if you please."

\*

Katie waited in the tiny scullery with bated breath. She had sent the boys to the nursery with strict instructions not to come down until the coast was clear. She tried to finish the dishes, but she dropped a plate in her distress and watched it shatter on the floor into dozens of pieces.

*Tom. Wanting to see her. Tom. In the British Army.*

She dropped to her knees and started picking up the broken pieces. Her fingers were wet and soapy and in her distress, Katie was clumsy. She picked up several jagged pieces before she realized she'd cut her finger. Her heart had been aching so much, she hadn't even noticed the pain. She shuddered, feeling the sharp sting of the cut now, and wrapped her finger tightly in her apron, not wanting to see the blood. Katie struggled to dispel images of her own blood on the blanket that night in the station. The night she gave birth to Tom's baby.

Then she heard Michael's voice.

"Katie?"

She stifled a sob. "I'm in here. Has he gone?"

"Yes. Come out here, Katie. I can't possibly get this bloody thing in there."

She emerged, and he gestured her to sit on one of the kitchen chairs.

"Do you want me to tell you what he said?" Michael asked.

"Yes. Tell me everything."

\*

She only had to ask at the post office, they would know where he was staying. There were only the two places anyway—the hotel by the golf course or the Dog and Whistle. Katie's money was on the hotel, as Tom had always been a bit of a snob, but it turned out he was at the Dog and Whistle.

She wished she could have walked in there anonymously, but there was no escaping the fact that the whole village was about to know her business. It would, undoubtedly, get back to Michael.

The bartender directed her to the snug, where Tom was having a jar. He looked different in uniform. It suited him. That khaki green color went well with his dark hair. He rose to his feet when he saw her and set his beer on the mantelpiece.

"Katie! Thank heavens you've come. I'm leaving on the first train to London tomorrow."

His blue eyes twinkled like the Irish Sea, and he bent to give her a kiss. Just a chaste peck on the cheek, but she caught a whiff of the beer he'd been drinking, and his six o'clock shadow grazed her face. He was the sort of man who needed to shave twice a day to stay really smooth.

"Tom." She could not inject much warmth into her greeting, but the emotion rose high when she asked the next question. "What on earth possessed you to volunteer?"

"Better than staying at home, missing all the fun."

"Fun?" Katie said, spitting the word like a curse.

"A chance to travel, see the world."

"You have hated the British all your life, and now you are going to fight in their war for them? For fun? For a chance to see a hole in the ground and your blood and guts spilled just before you fall into it?"

"That's no way to speak to a man who wasn't afraid to stand up and shoulder a gun."

"What about running your father's business, making changes like you told me in your letter. Have you left your mother to cope with all that?"

"She's got Dervla."

"Your sister is ten years old, Tom!"

"I needed to spread my wings," he said. *As if he were a restless angel.*

She sighed, and changed the subject. "Why are you here?"

"To see my heart's own darling," he said, with a twinkle in his eye and a bit of a grin playing about his lips.

"Don't, Tom," she said. "I know you well enough now not to fall for it."

His face suddenly became serious, as he obviously thought to try a different tack. "We need to talk, Kathleen."

Katie knew the reason. "You want to hear about the child."

A man likes to know, when his life's in danger, if he's got a son or a daughter to leave behind."

"You left that chance behind a long time ago."

"I'm only asking if it was a boy or a girl, Katie"

She reeled away from him. *Her own little girl. Tiny little hands and feet. Her hair, in damp curls, stuck to her tiny fragile head.*

"I can't talk about it, not even to you."

"Hey, Katie, love. You've gone as white as a sheet," he said. "Sit down and I'll get you a drink."

Hastily, anxiously, he made a place for her by the fire, and she let him push her down onto the seat. There was real concern on his face, and her attitude toward him softened. He checked the change in the pocket of his new khaki trousers before heading to the bar. Katie watched him go, shambling along in his army boots, and she felt sick at heart. He leaned forward on the bar, his large frame looking out of place.

He looks like a brute, thought Katie, so different from Michael in almost every way. A handsome brute though.

Tom returned with a gin and tonic, the drink he used to buy for her back in their hometown. Mother's ruin, Katie thought immediately. It's what you were supposed to drink if you didn't want the baby.

But she had wanted her baby, desperately. If only Tom had faced up to his responsibilities and asked her to marry him, she could have given birth in Ireland, kept her little baby and watched her grow.

Tom's fingers touched hers as he passed her the drink.

"I think I made a stupid mistake letting you go, Katie.

"I think you did, too."

"We need to discuss things properly. I've got a room upstairs." She shook her head. "I'm not going up there with you."

"Finish your drink. Then we'll talk."

*

Michael rolled into the kitchen where Roy was sitting alone at the kitchen table, struggling with his homework. It was unusually quiet and tranquil, apart from the occasional epithet from Roy's lips as he frowned his way through a long list of words to learn for a spelling test tomorrow.

"Where is everyone?"

"The little kids are in bed, and Alfie's just gone up, too, with one of your old comic books. Hope you don't mind."

"Not that much," said Michael.

He had a look over Roy's shoulder. The boy's method of committing words to memory was to write them out, over and over again in the back of his rough book with a heavy, inky hand.

"Where's Katie? She usually helps you with that, doesn't she?"

"Dunno. Sorry." The answer was meant to sound nonchalant, but it immediately rang alarm bells for Michael, who knew the sound of a cover-up when he heard one.

"Her hat and coat are not on the hook," Michael observed. "Roy? Where's Katie?"

Roy looked up and gave a sigh. "Gone out."

"At this time of night? On her own?"

"Well, I don't think she'll be on her own for long, mister. She went to the Dog and Whistle."

"She's gone to see O'Brien?"

Roy gave up the pretense and shut his book. "You should go after her, Mister Lord. Don't let that paddy fella get her."

Michael stared at the boy. A great, ugly looking fellow he was going to be with his shaggy dark curls and his chubby face. It would be easy to believe Roy had some gypsy blood in him. "If only it was as easy as that."

"Well, just wait then. He'll be stopping bullets before long, won't he? Maybe one of us will get her in the end."

It always came as a shock to Michael when Roy said something that clearly indicated that he saw himself as a *rival* for Katie's affections.

"Don't pass judgments on things you don't understand, young man."

"I understand you'll let her slip through your fingers unless someone puts a grenade underneath you. Do you want me to take you down there so you can get her back?"

"What?"

"You've got petrol in the car," said Roy. "I could wheel you out there, stick you in the car, and we could be down at the Dog and Whistle in no time."

Michael was silent for a moment, thinking fast. The idea rather appealed to him. "Can you drive a car, Roy?"

"I drove a van once in London. I drove it fast too, coz it was nicked."

Michael felt a flare of surprise, but then accepted this tidbit philosophically. He should have known with Roy. "There won't be much traffic on the roads, so I suppose we could risk it."

"Grab your hat and scarf then, Mister, and we'll get going. At least she'll see that you mean business."

\*

Katie knew she shouldn't have agreed to go upstairs with Tom. But how could she tell him about their little girl when it seemed the whole village had turned out downstairs—boozy old men telling jokes and wheezy stories, laborers throwing darts and spilling beer on the floor, village busybodies listening in.

Tom's room was much too small for a big, loose-limbed chap like him. It was an attic room, with a low sloping ceiling, and a little gabled window. Katie felt safer in front of it, looking across the green and through the trees to a nice view of the river beyond. It would be getting dark soon.

She turned back and glanced awkwardly at Tom, who seemed lost for words, too.

Tom sat down on the bed and patted the space beside him.

"I'm all right where I am," she said stiffly.

So Tom joined her at the window, stooping to look out over the village green.

"Lovely place," he observed. "I shall think about you here in this peaceful place while I'm in the war. Will you write me?"

She didn't want to say yes, but wasn't sure she ought to say no, either. What harm would a few letters do?

Except that she hated receiving his letters, full of mixed messages and references to broken promises. Instead, she skirted his question.

"Where will they send you?" she asked.

"How would I know? I suppose it won't be Greece now. I'd rather have liked a look at Greece."

Katie smiled. That was the Tom she had known in Ireland. Full of mad schemes to see the world and enjoy himself at somebody else's expense.

He was right behind her now. He put his hands on her shoulders and she didn't stop him. He was an old friend, and perhaps he did have a prior right. Seeing him made her realize how out of place she was here in this English village and even more so at Farrenden Manor with Michael. Who was she trying to fool? Herself?

She could feel Tom's body close to hers, though she would not turn around to embrace him. She could feel him leaning closer, his warm breath on the side of her face, and she sensed the very moment when he decided to lower his lips onto the curve of her neck.

*

The red sports car drew up right outside the Dog and Whistle.

"I'll go inside and find her," Roy said as he jumped out and dashed into the pub. Michael had no choice but to wait in the passenger seat, since they had left the wheelchair at home.

Roy was gone for about ten minutes, while Michael waited impatiently wishing like hell he had not entrusted any part of this mission to a surly, twelve-year-old boy. He should never have allowed Roy to interfere in his troubled romance with Katie, if that's what it was. Michael glanced uneasily at the pub, with its jolly hanging baskets of flowers and its shabby thatched roof. The old gray straw was shedding in places, making the place look like it needed a trip to the barber. Michael sighed. Could he, with any degree of legitimacy, say that he was *romantically involved* with Katie? His feelings had run high when he met that O'Brien fellow, that's for sure.

He must be. Romantically involved, that was.

Roy came hurrying out of the pub alone and Michael frowned as he leaned over the door to hear the news.

Roy's face was grave. "She's gone upstairs with him, Mister."

Michael swallowed hard and glanced away. "Dear God."

"Shall I ask the landlord to go upstairs and tell her you're out here waiting? Or do you want to try to get in there yourself?"

Michael stared at the walnut dashboard, as if the answer should be written there for him. "I can't face people laughing at me. And I don't want that Tom fellow to know I can't walk."

"So you're gonna just wait here until she comes out," Roy challenged. "What if she's in there the whole night?"

Michael glanced up at the inn's gabled windows. He knew

where the guest rooms were—he'd been there with a girl himself on more than one occasion. Roy glanced up, too, and they both saw the curtains being drawn in one of the upper rooms. They couldn't see the face, but the arm was definitely male.

"Bloody hell," Roy cursed. "She's in that room with him, sir!"

Michael gave a heavy sigh. He ran a hand over his face.

*Think fast, man, think fast.* That's what he always used to will himself to do when he was up above the clouds in his Hurricane.

*The enemy has made his next move clear—decide on a course of action and carry it out, straight away.* The image that came to Michael was of Katie, kneeling beside the broken plate on the scullery floor, tears in her eyes and drops of blood on the floor. She was scared of this man O'Brien, scared of the power this man had over her. And he would hurt her again if he got the chance.

"Come on, sir. Make a decision," Roy begged.

She needs rescuing, Michael realized, and he was the man to do it. If only he had his legs, he be in there in a trice. But he had to think laterally now.

"Honk the horn," he instructed Roy.

"What?"

"Just sound the horn, for heaven's sake!"

But Roy still looked flummoxed and Michael became impatient. He reached over, and started squeezing the horn like the whole village was on fire.

The landlord came running out, wiping his hands on his linen apron. "Do you need me to bring you a drink, sir?"

"No," said Michael, still blasting away on the horn. "I'm trying to attract my housemaid's attention."

People came to the doorway while others stared out the tiny windowpanes. Some stopped what they were doing on the village green to stare in amazement.

"Looks like you've got the attention of the whole bleedin' village," Roy observed.

The landlord wiped sweat off his anxious forehead and gave Michael a bewildered look "Your housemaid, sir?"

"Yes. She has been lured into your drinking establishment by a young Irishman of ill repute," Michael said with as much lordly aplomb as he could muster.

Roy tugged at Michael's sleeve. "Look, Mister, there she is. Up there!"

Katie stood in the window of the upper room, and was struggling to open the casement itself. She finally forced it free and leaned out. She clapped a hand over her mouth in surprise when she saw Michael, but she looked delighted to see him.

"Katie!" he yelled. "He's had his chance. He's not good enough for you, darling. Come away with me!"

She looked thrilled, and Michael saw her chest heave with emotion. She was tearful but vindicated.

They could all hear Tom in the background, the rise and fall of his Irish accent begging her not to make a fool of herself. They all saw Katie turn to him and ask, "So I can make myself into a fool with you instead?"

Katie's face reappeared at the window, and she waved at Michael and Roy. "I'm coming down, right now."

She appeared moments later, running across the yard outside the pub, with Tom O'Brien in hot pursuit.

"So, Kathleen. Is that how it is? Some rich bloke takes an interest—and all he has to do is beep his horn and you go running. It's all lies and promises, no doubt."

Katie turned to face her old flame, for what Michael hoped would be the last time. "You were the one good at the lies and promises, Tom. He hasn't made me any promises. But he's come to fetch me home."

Michael opened the passenger door. "Hop in then," he commanded. "Plenty of room if I budge up."

"I know. It isn't the first time we've had to share," Katie reminded him and flung herself into his arms. Michael gave her a rather flashy kiss. He knew perfectly well he was making a meal of her not just for himself, but for Tom.

Roy tooted the horn to get their attention again.

"Where to, milord?"

Katie was the one who answered. "Home, James, and don't spare the horses!"

# Chapter Sixteen

Michael sat at his desk, preparing to order some more horse feed so they wouldn't run out again. Determined to set the whole farm running like a well-oiled machine, as it had done in his father's time. It was a noble goal, but unfortunately, he was in no mood for it. Last night, he had felt on top of the world. The girl of his dreams had left that great dolt and stepped merrily into his car—into his arms, no less. She'd been overflowing with gratitude.

But this morning he was full a doubts and dark thoughts. What would she have done if Roy hadn't driven him to the village? Would she have managed to free herself from that man's clutches? He rather doubted it. Anyone could see that Katie still carried a torch for O'Brien, despite his appalling treatment. This morning, he'd watched Katie at breakfast this morning as he always did, and she had been absent-minded. When the radio broadcast came on with news about the war progress, she had turned up the wireless and paid a lot more attention than the day before.

She cared about Tom, that was obvious. Michael's stomach clenched. Perhaps she would have been touched deeper still in the bedroom at the Dog and Whistle if Michael hadn't interrupted things. He tossed his fountain pen down onto his desk. What did he care about running the farm when it was only pure luck that Katie woke up here at Farrenden instead of in the arms of her unreliable Irishman?

Michael hated luck. It was luck that he had landed on that roof and broken his back, and it was luck that he survived to tell the tale. Luck led him to meet Katie in the first place, and luck could just as easily steal her away from him again.

Unless he did something about it.

If he could only get well again he was sure she'd stay. And not just because she was sorry for him, either. If *he* could stand on his own two feet, strong and virile like Tom, then perhaps she would allow herself to fall in love again. He realized with a heart-searing pang through every part of his body that could still feel pain, that he longed for Katie to forget Tom and fall in love with him.

*

Katie was in the library on her hands and knees polishing the claw feet on the armchairs when she heard him call out for her. She sensed the anxiety in his voice—and something more, something like anger.

"Katie!"

Did he imagine she had nothing to do all day except to be at his beck and call?

"Katie! Come here this minute! I need to speak with you."

She abandoned the duster and the furniture polish and stood up. She untied the strings of her apron and threw it into the armchair, and then she ran along the hallway to his study.

"What is it, sir?"

He looked flustered as she came into the room. "Those papers we brought back from London. The ones the doctor gave us. Where are they?"

Katie hesitated. Lying was never her best talent. "I . . . can't remember, sir. Maybe Mrs. Jessop moved them."

"Don't be ridiculous. She's banned from my study since the incident with the ration books. You are the only person who's been in here except for me."

Katie bit her lip and didn't reply.

"Where have you put them?" he said, in a stern tone of voice.

She *knew* she couldn't answer him with a lie. "In the outside toilet, sir."

A look of shock flashed across his handsome face. "What?"

"I thought you'd finished with them. I . . . "

"But I need them, Katie. I want to telephone the surgeon today. I want this bloody back of mine sorted out."

"Now, sir. I don't think you should rush into anything. I don't think—"

His blue eyes widened. "You don't want me to do it. That's why you took the papers. You're hoping I'll forget all about it?"

Katie's heart thumped inside her. She knew how much the idea of getting better meant to him—however unrealistic it was. "Yes."

'You admit it?" He looked incredulous. "You hid the papers, on purpose?"

"Yes." She gazed back at him, trying to summon the courage to say what she needed to say. "There's too much risk involved, sir. You've recovered so well from your accident. Why tempt fate and take a gamble with your health now?"

"I'd gamble anything to be able to stand on my own two feet."

Katie gave a rueful laugh. "You would, would you?"

"Yes, I bloody well would. Think about it, Katie. Think how different my life could be."

"The doctor said the surgery might make things worse, Michael. I was there, remember? You asked me to be there."

"But, Katie. I want things to be like they used to be. I want—"

"I know what you want."

"Do you?" he said, bitterly. "I don't think so."

"Yes I do. You want to be the man you were before. You want to walk and run and impress everyone and go rushing back to win the war. But you're in love with a dream, sir."

He swallowed. "You don't think those things are possible?"

"No. I don't. I hate to be the one to break it to you," she said, wanting to go over to him and reach out and touch his troubled face, but not daring to. "But . . . you are kidding yourself, if you think the surgeons can work miracles. They're doctors, that's all, with hopes and dreams of their own. Maybe one day they'll be able to repair injuries like yours, and make people as good as new, but for now that's just a wild hope. They'd all like to be the first doctor to make a breakthrough. You're not a fool, sir. Don't go and be a guinea pig in some medical experiment. You are too important. Too valuable. Don't you see?"

He stared up at her with anguished blue eyes. Trying to make sense of what she was saying. "I'm useless, Katie. To you. To the war. To everyone."

"Don't say that!" The sound of her raised voice was a surprise, even to Katie, but she continued. "Don't say it, and don't think it, either. You are not useless. You have work to do the same as we all do. You have this huge farm to run."

"Hammond runs the farm. You know that."

"Hammond will run it into the ground if you don't watch out. He's too busy chasing skirt to care. You should stand up to him."

"Stand up to him?" Michael's face flushed with anger and bitterness. "Stand up to him! How the hell do I do that, exactly?"

"You know what I mean." Katie didn't know if she had the nerve to keep going, seeing him look at her like that. But she *had* to convince him. She had to talk him out of this. She owed him—for helping her out last night. She'd come so close to making a huge mistake with Tom and his lordship had saved her. She wanted to do the same for him. "For heaven's sake, you are twice the man that Hammond is. That Tom is. You proved that to me last night."

He blanched. They both knew that it cost her dearly to speak of her foolishness with Tom. But at that moment Katie would have said just about anything to convince him.

He nodded, as if grateful for her sacrifice, and his expression softened. "I always liked to be the one to save the day, Katie. And when I had my health and strength, it was easy to play the hero. These days, it's more difficult."

"You are the same man, sir. You can still win this war, but you're fighting on a different battlefield now. Forget the past. Find your strength and your courage and put them to good use. Please."

There was a long, long pause. Katie was terrified she'd overstepped the mark. He was not someone who took commands. He was someone who gave them. He could order her out of the house at a moment's notice. She waited for his anger to erupt, for his pride and his fear to get the better of him. But his tone of voice was quiet, when he finally spoke.

"I'll consider it."

"You promise?" she asked, softly.

"Yes."

*

Katie took the bus to Great Farrenden—where she knew there was a Catholic church. She heard mass for the first time since she got to Farrenden Manor and thought seriously about saying her confession. She hadn't let Tom touch her, but she had been tempted. It wasn't that she still loved Tom; in fact, she felt a fierce hatred for him. But he was part of her old life.

He was familiar, and he was all she had ever known. And he was her link with the little girl they had made in one of their brief, embarrassing trysts. Against the old oak tree, perhaps, or on the storeroom floor at Tom's parents' shop.

She felt a surge of shame that she had ever let Tom have his way with her, and vowed that things would be different from now on.

Not that she had been entirely successful in her resolve. She blushed at the thought of the scene outside the tavern. His lordship had put on a fine performance to help her escape Tom's clutches. She had played along with it, and was very grateful for the rescue. But that didn't mean that she and Michael were courting. Of course it didn't. That was unthinkable.

She knew full well that Michael took a very liberal, modern view of sex—one the priest at the alter would certainly not approve of, she reminded herself sharply. She knelt down on the uncomfortable bench in the church pew to pray for a strengthened resolve and to become a more dignified person than she had ever yet managed to be.

# Chapter Seventeen

Days went past, and Michael spent the best part of them sulking in his room. Katie knew he needed time, but the children were less understanding.

"Where's Mister Lord?" George kept asking, "I want to play dogfights on the front lawn, and it's no fun without him. Where is he?"

"In bed with a cold," Katie lied.

Roy was too cynical to accept that. "Nursing his sorrows with a bottle of cognac, last time I looked."

Katie gave him a hard stare to shut him up. "He's not feeling the best. He'll be up and about when he's ready."

She spoke with more confidence than she felt. She'd done her bit, and she'd said her piece. It was all a matter of waiting and hoping now.

On Thursday morning, Katie gathered up the mail from the past few days, and put it on his lordship's breakfast tray. She went upstairs and gave the letters to Michael. He leafed through them, and lighted on one that looked official.

"This one's from the RAF," he said, as he tore it open.

Then he fell silent, scanning the words in horror and disbelief.

"What is it?" she asked, afraid of the answer. To her dismay, he gave a kind of sob, and then his shoulders heaved and she knew he was crying.

"Get out!" he said.

"No," she said, fierce and determined. She snatched the letter off the bed and scanned the words herself. Discharge papers, as she suspected.

"For failing to fulfill the RAF physical requirements," she read. "Oh, Michael, I'm sorry." The words sounded woefully inadequate.

"Don't." His voice was hard and terse, while the tears glittered down his cheek. He made no effort to rub them away.

"It had to come sooner or later," she said.

"It's too soon. They haven't given me enough time."

She bit her lip. "It's an honorable discharge. You've done your bit."

"I wanted to do more, a lot more."

"You're already a hero," she said. "They mention recommending you for medals."

He grabbed the letter from her and started tearing it into pieces.

Katie tried to stop him, tried to fight him for it, but after a moment or two, the fight went out of him and she was able to hold him tightly in her arms.

"I don't want medals," he said, like a petulant child.

"I know," she said.

*

When she had gone, Michael lay staring at the canopy of the four-poster bed, watching the breeze ruffle the decrepit old tassels that edged the curtains.

"Mister Lord?" Alfie approached the bed, shyly, holding his notebook.

Michael sighed. "What is it, Alfie?"

"You know how you said you'll never fly again? Or dance, or ride a horse? I think I can solve the last one." Alfie proffered his sketchbook.

Michael took it, reluctantly, but he didn't flip it open. He wasn't in the mood for one of Alfie's inventions. He needed to concentrate on feeling miserable. But Alfie's eyes shone full of hope, and the glass lenses in his little round spectacles flashed as he hopped onto the bed, waiting for Michael to open the book and be amazed.

"Before I open this, let's get a few things clear. If this requires special equipment, large financial outlay or public embarrassment for me, I'm not likely to agree to it, do you understand?"

Alfie nodded, and licked his lips, still glancing hopefully at the notebook.

Michael opened the book. The drawing, rendered heavily in HB pencil, showed a contraption that might raise a broken man into the saddle. Alfie leaned forward and started bouncing on the bed in a quiver of anticipation.

"Steady on," said Michael. "I'm trying to have a proper look at this."

The idea was seductively simple. It worked using a system of pulleys, a strong cable, and a harness that went under the armpits of the brave (or foolhardy) person who wanted to ride.

"You see," Alfie said, almost breathless with enthusiasm, "we could raise you up onto the horse like a knight in shining armor."

Michael smiled. Who was he to tell Alfie that all those stories about knights being winched up onto their mounts were just myths and legends? Michael stabbed his finger at the sketch. "I'm assuming this bit has to be fixed fairly securely onto the stable roof?"

"No, sir. I've measured the stable roof, and it isn't high enough. We'd have to construct a framework outside in the yard."

Michael was doubtful, but he glanced again at the sketch and tried to imagine it. Alfie got his stubby pencil out of his pocket and snatched the sketchbook back. He licked his pencil and made a few adjustments.

After a moment, he handed it back to Michael, who scrutinized it carefully and gave a nervous laugh. "Ah, I see. A kind of gibbet, do you mean, for me to hang suspended above my horse?"

"You've got it, Mister."

Michael turned the sketch around and looked at it from every possible angle.

"Your eyes are glinting," said Alfie, with a smile.

*

Katie was counting the good silver, laying it out on a polishing cloth on the dining room table. She was surprised to see Michael dressed and wheeling himself about. An air of grim determination clung to him. She didn't understand it, but she was glad to see it.

"I need a length of rope, Katie, strong enough to hold my weight."

Katie heard the words and jumped to interpret his meaning. "Not a length of rope! Anything but that."

Michael gave an impatient snort. "Don't be ridiculous, Katie. Do you think I'd tell you if I was trying to kill myself?"

He plunked the sketch down on the dining room table for her to see. "We're building this. I've telephoned through to Hammond. He's bringing the wood."

Katie examined the sketch and rolled her eyes. "This is one of Alfie's ideas, isn't it?"

"Yes. A good one."

"It's a monstrosity. Drawn by a very unusual child. You can't be planning to put your safety at risk by trying it out, can you?"

Michael looked aloof. "I'm disappointed by your skepticism, Katie. I shall still need the rope on the terrace. Before lunch."

*

They hastily constructed the wooden framework in about an hour. Michael grasped one of the upright posts that supported the timber frame and tried to shake it. It wouldn't budge. It was a fine looking structure, made of sweet-smelling new pine, oozing resin here and there. They had bolted it to a fencepost for extra security. He smiled.

"Seems firm enough, Hammond."

"She's solid as a rock, sir."

Alfie and the twins hopped around in excitement, while Roy leaned against the fence, pretending to be much too grown-up to be interested.

At last it was time to try it out. Michael took off his sports jacket and flung it over the arm of his wheelchair. Alfie approached holding a coil of rope and Michael slipped it over his head and under his arms. He tested to make sure it was secure.

Slowly, with infinite care, the group lifted him. Michael rose up off the chair with his legs dragging behind him as if they belonged to a lifeless rag doll. He hated the look, but forced the vain thoughts out of his head to enjoy the moment.

Alfie clapped his hands in glee. "I told you it would work!"

Then one of the twins piped up. "But . . . why isn't he wearing the shining armor?"

"It would weigh him down, you idiot!" Roy snarled. ""Michael writhed uncomfortably—the harness was pinching his chest. Roy saw him and ran forward to adjust it, forgetting all about the rope. It whizzed through the pulley and Michael fell. He landed back in his chair with a bone-jarring thump that resonated through all the parts of his body.

He groaned and cursed the child for his stupidity.

A rather penitent Roy rushed to his side. "Are you all right, sir?"

"You let go!" Michael said, in outrage. "You bloody idiot."

"You're all right then, nothing broken?"

"Nothing new. Only my bloody back. My surgeon would have a fit if he could see this!"

Katie's anxious face peered out the window, her hands covering her mouth, and her eyes round with alarm.

Michael refused to be beaten. "Come on lads, let's give it another try, shall we? This time we'll get it right."

Roy jumped to grab the end of the rope. This time Roy and Hammond hauled together, and Michael rose again into the air. The rope chafed under his arms and around his chest, though he had worn an old sweater.

"This is bloody agony!" he yelled. "I'm going to ask for modifications, if we ever attempt this again."

Michael was suspended in midair, long legs dangling below.

Somehow the rope had twisted, and now it decided to untwist. Michael found himself turning midair in a circle. He enjoyed a unique three hundred and sixty degree view of the stable yard before finally settling above the horse—facing toward her tail. The nag decided to emphasize the moment by lifting said tail and letting a prodigious quantity of horse manure cascade onto the cobblestones below.

"Look out!" yelled Roy, as the twins stepped smartly out of the way and stood gazing in horrified amazement at the steaming pile of dung.

"Oh my Gawd," said Bob.

"Phew! Can you smell that stench?" said George.

"Why is it green?" Alfie asked.

"Excuse me," Michael interrupted. "Now that we've all admired Midnight's little offering, can we concentrate on the task in hand? I'm suffering from terrible rope burn up here!"

Hammond took the strain, as Roy took hold of Michael's legs and twirled him round in a rather casual manner.

"Don't let go, or I'll be back to square one again," ordered Michael. It took a while to get him into just the right spot, but at last they accomplished it.

"Lower away," Michael commanded, glancing across to see if Katie was still watching—hoping she'd witness his moment of triumph.

"Wait a minute," said Roy, trying to prevent Midnight from wandering away. "Get underneath him, there's a good girl."

Michael looked down. The wretched beast wasn't cooperating, and she had a look of horsy disdain on her face.

"Gently, Roy. Don't pull on her mouth. She hates that," he instructed, from above. "Alfie? Why don't you try? She doesn't like bullies."

Alfie shook his head. "I'm not going near her, Mister. She don't like me at all. Look at her, giving me the evils!"

Michael sighed, fearful of another bumpy landing on the cobblestones.

So again Roy swapped places so that Hammond, a man who understood the workings of a horsy brain, could coax Midnight back into position.

"Hurry," Michael urged. The rope clutched him around the chest like a boa constrictor and he feared any minute now he would admit defeat and demand release.

Finally, they lowered Michael down onto his horse, and a cheer went up in the stable yard. Michael shrugged off the rope, cursing a little, and pulled down his sweater where it had ridden up. He leaned forward and patted Midnight's neck to reassure her.

"It's me old girl. Back in the saddle. You'd like to go for a canter, wouldn't you?"

"Is that wise, sir?" Hammond put Michael's right foot in the stirrup for him, and then glanced up at his lordship with concerns. "You won't have the control you used to have . . . "

Michael stared at him coolly until the man glanced away. Hammond didn't apologize for questioning his master, but he went round to the other side of the horse, and with a kind of mock obedience, he placed Michael's left foot in the stirrup, and stood back.

His heart already racing with anticipation, Michael made a clicking sound in the back of his throat.

"Walk on," he demanded, and Midnight lumbered into action. Michael shortened the reins and checked to see if Katie was still watching, which of course, she was.

Michael smiled and inclined his head, proudly, as if setting out for the show-jumping arena. The horse's hooves clicked across the yard and out toward the paddock.

"Not too fast or you'll be thrown, sir," called Alfie.

But Michael trusted Midnight. With a sort of breathless, rising excitement, he tapped with his hand on her flank where he would have used the pressure of his knee in the old days.

"Go on, girl, they can't stop us now," he urged. She needed no more encouragement. He felt that incredible power ripple beneath him, and the horse took flight across the hillside in huge easy bounds, while Michael's heart soared with her. He clung tight and let Midnight take him for the ride of his life. "Horsepower!" he bellowed.

He reveled in the feel of her warm coat under his fingers; the smell of the wet, damp earth; the thundering sound of hooves as they raced across the field. She's roaring like my old Hurricane, he thought, as he leaned forward and laughed. He headed for the little stand of trees and did a circuit around them. He tried out everything he dared to do without losing his balance. He found that it was perfectly possible to ride, and ride well, even without the use of his legs.

He returned to the yard breathless and euphoric. The children were all sitting in a row on the fence, watching him closely. Alfie looked particularly pleased with himself. The twins were bobbing their heads in excitement and even Roy seemed flushed with success.

"Alfie, you're a genius," he said. "I could take care of the whole farm like this. I could check up on things every morning from horseback. Wouldn't that be something?"

Everyone agreed heartily—all except for Hammond, who looked rather dismayed.

*

The escapade put Michael in a good mood as he rolled in for tea with the children. "Make way," he teased, as he took up his duties at the head of the table.

He's beginning to accept it, Katie thought. He's beginning to see what he *can* do, instead of what he can't. She smiled, and he smiled back.

Michael turned to Alfie and ruffled his hair. "If it doesn't rain tomorrow, I could take you lot out on the lake," he said.

Katie looked up sharply.

"In a boat?" said Bob.

"Yes."

"Sir, are you sure that's . . . " Katie stopped. She was going to say "wise," but she thought better of it. "Are you sure that's what you want to do?"

"Yes," Michael said, the lordly tone coming back into his voice. "It is. I haven't been rowing for ages. You're not worried about the children's safety, are you?"

"I didn't say that," she replied. No. But she thought it. Four highly excitable kids in a rowing boat with a madcap lord? Could there be a better recipe for disaster? Honestly, ever since she'd given Michael that talking to about being sorry for himself he'd been turning into a right daredevil.

"Good God, Katie, I was the champion of the rowing team three consecutive years. The trophies are in the other room."

Roy looked up with interest at that.

Reluctantly, Katie could see she must muster some enthusiasm for Michael's plan. "Have you got life preservers?"

"For heaven's sake," Michael laughed. "It's been as calm as a millpond today. If it's like this tomorrow, it'll be impossible to capsize. That rowboat is virtually unsinkable."

"Isn't that what they said about the Titanic?" Alfie said, and regretted it when he saw the look on Katie's face. "Sorry. I want to go, honest! We are still going, aren't we?"

"Are them trophies made of silver, Mister?" Roy chirped up, unexpectedly.

"Keep your mitts off my trophies, Roy," Michael said. "Yes. We're going on the lake tomorrow. Agreed?"

"Agreed," Katie murmured, like saying amen at the end of a prayer. Which is what she would be doing every minute that those kids were out on that lake with Michael.

# Chapter Eighteen

Michael relaxed in the stern of the boat, lying back against some old cushions they found in the summerhouse. It was warm and he trailed his fingers lazily over the side and into the water. This was bliss.

He smiled. Katie was right, as ever. He was lucky to be alive, and there was more to life than sulking about his legs. Someday he'd like to thank her.

After they'd been afloat about twenty minutes, Bob got fidgety and wanted to sit next to his brother. Roy, of course, didn't want to relinquish his place near the front. Naturally Bob stood up to protest, and then tried to squeeze himself onto the seat beside George, wobbling the boat. The splash was almost inevitable. Bob was in the water, and the remaining children made things worse by leaning over the side, stretching out their hands for him to grab on to. The boy gasped and panicked in the water.

"Sit down or we'll capsize," Michael yelled. They all seemed to be screaming at the tops of their voices, and George was frantic with fear. "Bob can't swim! Mister! Do something!"

There was but one course of action open to Michael under the circumstances. He let out a sigh of resignation, almost boredom, and flipped himself over the back of the boat and into the water. It was a most peculiar sensation diving into the water. Michael hadn't swum since before his accident, and though he couldn't kick with his feet, he found that he could swim pretty well using his arm strength. The noise of the water made a rushing sound in his ears, and a corresponding rush of adrenalin coursed through his body. *I still love the water.*

His arms swooped back as he swam under the boat—the quickest way to get to the boy. His hair streamed from his face.

Above him, light filtered through the murky water, and he was faintly aware of the children's voices, muffled and distant. Michael swam upwards now, toward the surface until he reached the boy.

He had Bob in his arms in an instant, and they both surfaced, splashing and gasping. He caught hold of the boat with his free hand, and tried to get Bob to heave himself on board, but the little child clung, terrified, to Michael.

"Drag him up, Roy, for heaven's sake. George and Alfie, don't move—we need you to balance Roy's weight."

As they hauled Bob onboard sopping wet, his waterlogged shorts fell down, revealing, to Michael's shock, that Bob was a little girl. Bob hauled up his—no, her—pants as soon as she was aboard the boat, but it was too late.

Michael laughed out loud. It certainly was a week of surprises. He swam to the back of the boat, wondering how he would manage to climb back in. Luckily, Roy's help and his own strength were sufficient.

Bob was hysterical. "Don't send me back, Mister. Please don't send me back."

Michael looked at the little waif, shuddering in the front of the boat. "Why would I send you back?" Michael asked.

"Coz you said you didn't have no room for girls here," Bob said.

Michael had not in fact had anything to do with the decision to send only boys to Farrenden Manor. That had been Mrs. Mallory's idea.

"I take it your name isn't Bob?" Michael enquired, sardonically.

"Back in Stepney, it was short for Roberta."

To Michael, her pronunciation of *Roberta* sounded like a threat on the lips of a London thug, but he kept that thought to himself.

"Thank you, sir," said George. "For rescuing my sister."

Michael rowed back to the shore. His wet shirt stuck to his arms, his trousers were covered in bits of pondweed, and he was sitting in a pool of water, but he couldn't have been happier.

As they rowed back to the jetty, the children filled him in on the story.

It had been Alfie's idea, of course. While waiting for a billet with all the other evacuees, he had noticed that siblings of opposite sexes were split up. The twins couldn't bear the idea of being separated, so Alfie suggested they disguise Bob as a boy. Roy filched the scissors from Mrs. Mallory's desk, and they chopped off Roberta's hair and flushed it down the toilet, which caused the mysterious blockage that day in the village hall.

"We felt a bit guilty about that," Alfie explained, "but it couldn't be helped."

"No, no. The end justifies the means," Michael interjected. "Tell me the rest."

The children hid Bob's suitcase behind a gravestone in the churchyard next door, and dressed her up in her brother's spare clothes. Then came the hard part: remembering to say *he* instead of *she*.

"George was useless," Alfie said. "I told him not to speak at all if he couldn't get it right."

"I've only just got the hang of it, and now I have to change back," George grumbled.

"I could stay as a boy, honest," Bob offered. "I like my school uniform. I don't want to wear no stupid dress."

"Them clothes cost a lot of money," George said. "It would be a waste if she had to have a dress."

There was a sort of poetic logic in their rash course of action that rather impressed Michael. "I think Katie will be interested to hear all of this," he said, as they pulled up the boat alongside the jetty. He was rather looking forward to telling her.

The despised wheelchair was there, tied to one of the mooring posts so it couldn't go anywhere. Michael frowned when he saw it. The incredible freedom he had felt in the water was still in his veins. He didn't want to be stuck in that thing again.

\*

Katie came running down from the house to meet them. She had witnessed the whole thing from an upstairs window: the children rocking the boat, one child flipping overboard, Michael throwing himself in the water. She'd been helpless through the kafuffle to do more than watch it unfold. She'd stayed where she was, holding her breath, until Michael had got Bob back in the boat. In fact, she'd held it a little longer, until she was sure that Bob was breathing. Only then did she spare a thought for Michael, the hero of the hour.

"It was a fine thing you did, sir, jumping in to get him," Katie knelt down and scooped Bob into her arms and told him what a naughty boy he was, until Michael pulled at Katie's arm and whispered something in her ear.

"No!" she said.

"Yes," Michael insisted. "I have seen the evidence with my own eyes."

"Are you sure, sir? Maybe you thought you saw something you didn't."

"Don't be ridiculous, Katie. I know the difference between a stallion and a mare. This used to be one of the finest stud farms in the country, and though a horse's anatomy is *slightly* different, I can assure you that young Bob here is a little filly." He glanced at the surly child standing on the jetty, and smiled.

Katie was astounded. "And she's hidden it all this time."

"Very unobservant of you, Miss Rafferty," Michael said, grinning at Bob. "Not to spot that one of your charges is a girl— and a very pretty little girl at that!"

Bob smiled shyly at Michael, and that clinched it for Katie. The tyke was a self-conscious young lady receiving her first compliment, without a doubt.

"But why, for heaven's sake?" Katie wanted to know.

"To be with her brother, of course," Michael said. "Twins. Unbreakable bond and all that."

Katie felt a bit of a fool.

*

By mealtime it was obvious something was wrong with Michael. At first, Katie thought he was brooding. He was very quiet during the meal and hardly touched his food, though chicken in wine sauce was one of his favorites. Katie was busy with the children after supper, but she resolved to go and find him after they'd gone to bed to see if she could work out what was wrong.

She found him in his library, poring over a medical journal full of articles about spinal injuries. He was hunched up in his chair, pale and shivering.

"Oh sir! Are you all right?"

"I don't know," he admitted. He tossed the medical journal aside disconsolately.

Tentatively, Katie touched a hand to his forehead. "You have a fever."

"Do I? I don't feel hot, though. I feel cold."

"You're sickening for something," she said. "You should go to bed."

"Will you come with me?" he said, but his eyes betrayed his exhaustion, and his smile was weak and faint.

She pursed her lips, and tried to make light of his remark. "Share your bed and catch the dreaded lurgy? No thanks, sir."

"Seriously Katie, I need your help just to get to the other room, I'm afraid."

That didn't sound good. All the fight seemed to have gone out of him along with the light in his eyes. "I'll tuck you in," she said, softly. "Of course I will."

# Chapter Nineteen

He shivered as she helped him undress. Tenderly she undid his necktie, and set aside his gold tiepin. He watched her affectionately as she undid the buttons down the front of his shirt and slipped it off his arms.

He lay back on the bed and let her undo the button-fly that fastened his trousers. Her fingers were quick and efficient. He gave her a regretful smile, and placed his hand on top of hers for a moment, to slow her down.

"I've often imagined you doing that."

"I daresay you have, sir, but you're in no fit state to flirt with me now."

She dragged off his pants in a business-like manner and he almost convulsed with the cold. Beads of perspiration stood on his chest and his skin was pale. His whole body shivered and he was grateful when she fetched his dressing gown.

"Shall I ask the doctor to come up to the house"?"

"Certainly not. I don't want that arrogant know-it-all prodding and poking me around."

"I think you need the doctor, sir."

"I'll be the judge of that. You are not to call him without my express instructions. It's nothing. Just cover me up and I'll sleep it off."

Katie pulled the covers out from underneath him, then she hauled them up and over his freezing form to tuck them around his sides.

"I'll check on you in an hour," she announced, as if he had no say in the matter.

"I should like that," he said, and managed a grin, but then he groaned. His head was throbbing, and his bones ached. It hurt when he tried to move and it was easier to keep still.

\*

Katie knocked on the door an hour later, but his lordship didn't reply. She took her courage in her hands and pushed her way inside. He was worse, restless and burning with fever. He didn't even notice when she laid her hand on his forehead. His dressing gown had fallen open and his whole body was clammy and pale.

She ran to soak flannels in a bowl and sponge his face. First, she would cool him off, and then she was ringing for the doctor despite his instructions.

She tried to get him to drink something, but the way his head lolled away from her when she raised the cup to his lips set warning bells ringing. This wasn't just a common cold. She sponged him over once more, afraid to leave him even to make the telephone call. Nevertheless, she slipped into the hall, picked up the large polished receiver and asked for Dr. Larchwood's number.

"Please hurry," she said, when the man came on the line. "I don't know what's wrong with him. I've never seen someone go downhill so fast."

The doctor arrived twenty minutes later, his worn leather bag in his hand. Katie showed him to Michael's room and watched in high anxiety while he poked and prodded, just as Michael had predicted. Maybe it was just as well that he was oblivious to it all.

The doctor's face was lined and inscrutable, but when he asked her to step into the hallway, Katie's heart sank. When that happened back in Ireland, it was usually time to call for the priest.

Larchwood spoke in a low voice. "It's possible he may continue to get worse."

"I'll nurse him," she said. "But you need to tell me what to do."

"My dear girl. His accident weakened him—and it's been less than a year since it happened. He's been trying to do too much, too soon. His upper body may be strong but he's as thin as a rake, and being confined to a wheelchair means that his circulation isn't as good as it used to be. I have to warn you, Katie, this fever might be too much for him."

Katie almost covered her ears with her hands, like a little child who doesn't want to hear the truth. "No."

"He's been so unhappy since his accident, he might just slip away. It might be easier on him."

"No," she growled. "What kind of a doctor are you? He's a young man of twenty-six with his whole life ahead of him, and you think it would be better if he died!"

"Katie, what kind of life can he realistically have?"

"A good life. A fine life."

"What happiness can he have? He's been as close to misery as a man can be for months."

"Not lately, doctor. He's been much happier. And the children adore him." Katie wanted to say that she adored him, too, but she didn't quite have the courage.

"I daresay they do, but he still seemed very melancholy to me last time I saw him as a patient. You're a kind-hearted girl, and you value life highly, which is all to your credit. But he's weak and tired. Take yourself up to bed, and try to get some sleep, but prepare for bad news in the morning."

"No." Katie heard her own voice ringing out, threads of desperation clinging to its echoes. Fear of losing Michael gave her the courage to grab the doctor by the lapels and shout in his face. "Get yourself back in that room, Dr. Larchwood. Whatever drugs you have in that bag that might save him, show me how to give them to him. Whatever it takes to keep him alive, we'll do it."

Still Larchwood hesitated. "My dear girl. Don't get so upset." He tried to placate Katie, but she refused to listen.

"You have to help him!" she screamed, and she shoved the doctor through the doorway of Michael's bedroom.

Michael stirred and gave a kind of disturbed murmur of pain when the two of them crashed into the room. It had a sobering effect on both Katie and the doctor. Dr. Larchwood frowned and felt Michael's brow.

"He's in the grip of a fierce fever. I can only do what I can."

Katie looked up at him sharply. "As long as you *are* doing what you can, doctor, I shall be happy."

They worked on Michael all the evening. The doctor set up a saline drip to keep the fluids up and he taught Katie how to check the drip line and administer injections every two hours. Together they tried to make Michael more comfortable, and all the while, he slipped in and out of a feverish, delirious sleep. Katie soaked the warm flannels in cold water and washed the sweat from him endlessly.

Dr. Larchwood observed her from a chair by the fireplace. "You were in nursing, in Ireland?"

"I was meant to be, but things didn't turn out as I planned."

"You would have made an excellent nurse," he said. "Tenacious, quick to learn, compassionate."

Katie was silent. She did not admit that it was more than compassion that motivated her now—much more.

At half past two in the morning, Dr Larchwood announced he was going home.

Katie was panic-stricken. "You can't leave me here alone. The crisis hasn't passed."

"Fever doesn't reach a crisis, Katie. And we've done everything we can to make him comfortable."

"I don't want him to be comfortable; I want him out of danger. You'll be well paid, for heaven's sake. Stay and help me nurse him."

Dr. Larchwood shook his head. "I have to sleep sooner or later, my dear. I have other patients who will need me in the morning."

"Then leave me what I need for the drip."

Larchwood nodded his agreement.

He laid out the supplies, placing them in order along the top of the French-polished side table. Then he turned to go.

His hand was on the brass doorknob when he turned back to speak to Katie. "He's lucky to have such a loyal friend to guard his life."

"It isn't luck, it's irony." Katie's tone of voice was grim. "He saved my life once, and I wasn't grateful. I regret that now, and I must fight for his life in return."

*

Another hour later, Michael was still delirious.

"Michael, can you hear me? Stay with me. Please, don't give up," she begged.

She sank down onto the bed beside him. His eyes were half-closed, but she thought she saw a flicker of recognition. She took hold of his shoulders and shook him, trying to help him stay conscious, trying to get him to stay with her. His hold on life seemed fragile and she was terrified he would let go.

He murmured something so softly that she almost missed it, but she thought it sounded like, "Forgive me." A pang of terror went through her, a sharp scythe of fear.

"No! I'll never forgive you if you leave me, do you hear?" She stroked the hair back from his forehead with the damp flannel. The cool water seemed to bring him some relief, and his blue eyes flickered open as he struggled to focus on her face. "Oh, Michael. This is all my fault."

"Not your fault," he murmured. "Katie . . . I wanted you . . . so much . . . but I . . . can't walk . . . never will."

She started to cry. "I don't care what you can't do. I'm in love with you, and I have no choice in the matter. I love everything about you, including your disability, and that's the truth."

"Katie . . . " his breathing was shallow and rasping, and she was filled with a panicky sense of desperation.

It was time to play her trump card, no matter how much it cost her. "I remember you," she said. "That night in London, when you carried me down to the shelter. You saved me. You know you did." She scanned his face. She wasn't sure if he heard her or not, but it had to be said. This was the confession she couldn't give the priest.

"You saved me, sir, that night in the Tube station, and you gave me a life worth living here in this house with you. Please, my lord . . . *my love* . . . let me save you. I'll die of grief if you leave me!"

"Katie?" he said and his eyes opened. He touched the side of her face. His fingers were trembling and clammy.

She leaned forward, yearning to hear him speak. "I can hear you."

He twisted his face into a smile, with a huge effort. "Too tired . . . forgive me."

Katie was frantic. *He doesn't care if he lives or dies!*

There was nothing else she could try—the doctor's drugs would either do their work, or they wouldn't. Katie's heart was heavy, and she was tired, too. She lay down on the bed beside him, exhausted and wrung out.

She curled up on the bed beside Michael. She placed a protective hand on his chest, kidding herself that if his heart stopped beating, she'd feel it, even if she were asleep. She'd wake, she was sure she would, and she might just be able to revive him before it was too late.

*

Later, Katie was downstairs in the back scullery, emptying the enamel slop bucket down the drain as fast as she could to rush back upstairs to Michael.

Where there's life there's hope, she kept telling herself. It was a relief he had made it through the night. Dr. Larchwood was certainly surprised. He'd promised to call by again later, to help her to keep up the medications.

Bob appeared in the scullery, dressed for the first time as a little girl. "I want to show Mister Lord how I look, Katie. Can I?"

Katie straightened to look at Bob, who did look very adorable in her little short dress that showed her knees. Mrs. Jessop had managed to scrape her hair, short though it was, across to the side and hold it back by a clasp with a pink bow on top.

"He's very ill, Bob. As soon as he's well enough, I promise I'll take you up there, but not today."

Mrs. Jessop appeared in the doorway and the two women exchanged a silent conversation: Is he better? Mrs. Jessop's rheumy brown eyes answered in the negative. He could still die. And if he does, Katie thought, will you be the one to tell the little girl, or will I?

"It's because of me he took sick, isn't it?" Bob looked up with worried hazel eyes. "Because he jumped into the water."

Mrs. Jessop put a hand on Bob's shoulder, and spoke with unfamiliar gentleness to the little girl. "We'll go feed the chickens. You'd like to do that, wouldn't you, dear?"

And after they were gone, Katie finally allowed herself to wonder what would happen to them all if Michael didn't recover. She supposed they would all be sent to live their separate ways so the house could be sold.

*

Mrs. Mallory came to call and Katie let her look through the doorway at Michael, who had fallen into an uneasy, feverish sleep.

"He'll pull through," Mrs. Mallory insisted, though her face bore traces of doubt. "You must talk to him, tell him how much you want him to get better."

Katie gazed at Michael, too, worried by his pallid face and his ragged breathing. "I keep telling him, but I don't think he cares."

"He was like this after his accident. I was the only one at his bedside then. But it was you he spoke of."

"That's not possible, ma'am . . . "

"Katie, don't try to pretend any longer. He told me about that chance meeting in London and that he longed to know what had happened to you, so I made some inquiries on his behalf."

Katie's heart ached as she let the doorframe hold her weight.

Mrs. Mallory knew the whole story. And it was no coincidence that Katie had come to live at Farrenden Manor.

"He didn't need to trouble himself about me," Katie said, the tears coming fast now. "I was a stranger to him. A foolish girl—"

"A Titian-haired beauty. That's how he described you. Lit up by a terrible fire that blazed nearby. He told me that he took you in his arms and carried you down the stairs."

Katie nodded. "He saved my life."

"And he couldn't forgive himself for leaving you scared and in pain."

"I didn't expect him to stay," Katie protested. *She had wanted him to, though.*

"You have to remember, he was engaged to Connie at the time. Sometimes I think the only good thing to come out of his dreadful accident was that it scared that nasty woman away."

"You didn't like her?"

"No." Mrs. Mallory's lips pursed after she uttered that single syllable. "He deserved better."

Katie tried to blink away her tears. She needed to pull herself together.

Mrs. Mallory turned to go. "So now you know. What you choose to do with the information is up to you. I only hope you will find the courage to act upon it, my dear, if his life is spared."

*

Michael woke when the sunlight filtered into the room and touched his face. He turned his head, and saw her. She was lying asleep on the bed beside him. She lay on top of the eiderdown, and he was underneath, but they lay side by side. He reached out and pushed back some of the soft auburn curls, very gently, trying not to wake her. Her rosy lips parted a little, and she stirred but she did not wake.

*My beautiful Irish Kathleen.*

He lay for a long time watching her, wondering if he dared to kiss her but he knew she would wake if he tried such a thing. So he just lay there quietly, running over what he could remember of the last few hours. Had she really said that she loved him? Or was it just a dream brought on by the fever?

Just then, her eyes opened and widened in surprise.

"Forgive me, sir, I must have fallen asleep." She sat up and started rubbing her eyes to try to hide her embarrassment.

"Don't apologize. It feels good to wake up with a pretty girl in my bed."

She flushed.

Michael answered her with a smile. He knew she had no idea how good it felt. For many months, his first waking thoughts were on what the accident had taken from him. Today his thoughts were all for her.

She got up and strolled to the window to adjust the curtains so the glare wouldn't trouble him. She turned back, and he caught her eye. From the way she glanced away, he reckoned she was embarrassed. She *had* made those wild declarations of love, hadn't she? And now she was regretting it?

He ran a hand over his face in his anxiety, and felt a good growth of stubble. "How long have I been lying here?" he said in surprise.

"Three days," she told him. "We've all been beyond worried. I can't tell you how glad I am to see a change in you, sir. The doctor looks by every morning and he'll be pleased to see the improvement."

"You've been watching over me for three days?" Michael said, incredulously.

She nodded. "Mrs. Jessop's been taking care of the children so I could be up here with you. I always meant to be a nurse, back in Ireland, you see, so it seemed logical for me to do it. Dr. Larchwood showed me how to give you your injections."

Michael looked down and saw two little gauze dressings inside the crook of his elbow.

"I'm grateful," he said. His face burned a little at the thought of everything she must have done for him while he was ill. She stood by the bed like a novice nun, and with chaste, cool fingers, she touched his forehead.

"You're a little flushed but your fever's gone now," she said quietly as she adjusted his pillows. Her movements were quick and efficient—motherly even—but that wasn't what he wanted. He caught hold of both her arms, and held her wrists tight. He needed to hear her say it out loud, or force himself to hear the truth.

*You said you were in love with me. Did you mean it?*

But something stopped him. It was difficult to broach the issue now, in the cold light of day. It was obvious she didn't want to revisit the emotional outbursts of that feverish night. So instead, he resorted to flirting.

"Since we've spent the night together, why don't you give me a kiss?"

"You're obviously feeling better," she said crisply.

"I'd feel better still if I got a kiss," he insisted, and kept tight hold of her wrists.

His tactics didn't work on Katie. He ought to have known that by now.

"I have no intention of kissing you, sir. You haven't brushed your teeth for three days, and you're in desperate need of a shave," she said. "Let me go so I can fetch you some hot water."

Reluctantly, he released her, and she went over to the washbasin to find his shaving things.

"Katie?"

"Yes, sir?"

"I keep thinking of things that happened while I was ill."

He saw her face blanch and she bit her lip, and he felt a pang of guilt. His intention was not to embarrass her.

She brought the shaving things over and sat down on the bed to help him. She opened it up and smiled, and he realized she must have seen the little picture of Rita Hayworth that he kept tucked in there.

He took the little wooden box from her and closed it, firmly.

"I only want to thank you, that's all. Dr. Larchwood was difficult that first night, wasn't he? And you made him stay, I think."

"I wanted the very best treatment for you, sir. I did what my conscience told me to do."

"Your conscience," Michael said impatiently, "what about your heart?"

He saw her eyes fill with tears, and she tried to look away. Michael scowled. Why couldn't she say it? Why wouldn't she repeat what she'd said to him that night now that he was awake and able to respond?

\*

Katie went for a long walk down by the river. She needed to be alone with her thoughts. Yes, he had her heart, and now, he had the power to break it. What she felt for Michael was much deeper than any infatuation she had ever known before. This was real. She had thought she would die of heartbreak the night he nearly died in her arms.

She walked further, knowing that back at the house he would be sitting up in bed with the children crowded around him. They would be swarming all over the bed, happy and excitable. Bob would get her chance to show off her new dress, and all four of them would be thrilled to see their "squadron leader." Alfie would be talking about his inventions and George would be misunderstanding it all. Roy would be standing in the corner, taciturn on the surface, but happy all the same.

She was in love with him, yes, but what kind of future could there be for two people as different as her and Michael?

When she got back to the house, she decided to run herself a bath, recklessly ignoring the wartime guidelines to fill the tub only an inch or two deep. She let it fill up and up, and poured in a liberal amount of the bath crystals that she'd found in the back of the airing cupboard. After everything she had been through, she reckoned she deserved a good soak in a deep, foamy tub of hot water. But as she eased her body into the warm water and tried to relax, she could not dispel thoughts about what it might be like to love Michael—to really love him with her whole heart and her whole body. She took the small, precious piece of soap and used it liberally to wash away the troubles of the day, and all the time she wondered what it would be like to have his hands on her body. To feel his touch, his caress, instead of her own.

# Chapter Twenty

Katie checked to see if the corridor was empty before going to his room each night, not wanting the children to see her. She knew this was wrong. He wasn't ill any more, and the excuse that he might need her during the night was wearing a bit thin. Or rather, it had taken on an entirely different meaning.

Of course, they hadn't actually "consummated" their relationship. Katie still slept on top of the eiderdown, and Michael slept underneath. But it was different now. He would reach for her in the middle of the night, and they would kiss in the dark. His kisses left her weak with longing. Her desire to be close to him grew stronger all the time. The eiderdown barrier wouldn't last much longer.

"Katie! Is that you?" he called out.

"Yes, it's me," she said softly. She closed the door behind her. He was already in bed, and looking so pleased to see her that she felt her heart lurch. *This is wrong, this is all wrong.* Feeling as guilty as sin itself, she hovered by the door.

"Maybe you could turn the key tonight," he suggested, "so the children don't come in."

Katie was surprised. He had never asked for that before. But she did as he asked, and her fingers trembled as she turned the big heavy key in the door.

*I'm alone with him now, in a locked room.*

"Come here."

The space beside him on the bed beckoned to her, and so did his smile. No man should be allowed to have a smile like that, she thought. It must have won him dozens of admirers.

"Don't be shy," he said.

She nodded, but she couldn't speak. In the light of the bedside lamp, Michael's hair shone gold, and his eyes sparkled sapphire blue, for her. His aristocratic face was lean and handsome, and when he smiled again, she went weak.

He stretched out his hand. She sat on the very edge of the bed, feeling ridiculous and awkward. She wore a soft, brushed cotton, white nightgown and fiddled with the ribbon at the front,

"I'm wondering if I shouldn't go back to my own room, tonight."

A flicker of concern crossed his face. "I thought you quite liked being here with me?"

She put a hand to her chest. Her heart was beating much too fast. "You know I do."

"One more night, Katie. Just stay with me one more night."

"Mrs. Jessop knows."

"I don't care," he said.

Katie closed her eyes for a moment, overwhelmed by a yearning to be held tightly in his arms. "Lord Farrenden, I—" she began.

"Sweetheart! We are long past that!" He reached for her, impatiently, and pulled her close. His mouth was on hers and she trembled and gave in to his demanding kisses. She let him push her down on the pillows and kiss her throat, she let him fondle her breasts only to kiss her mouth again, deeper, harder as if he would bruise her lips, but then softer, sweeter, and more gentle than ever.

"You know I'm not a virgin," she said hesitantly, waiting for his reaction.

He stopped touching and stroking, and met her gaze instead.

"Katie, even if it had not been for that night we never talk about, I would have guessed. You have a knowing look about you."

She bit her lip. "Is that so?"

"Yes. I'd say that you have known pleasure at the hands of a man, but you have also known great pain."

He had hit a nerve and it was raw. She began to tremble. So this is what it felt like to have someone look into your soul.

He continued. "You trusted Tom, and then he hurt you."

She nodded.

"He was the reason you left," Michael said, watching her face without wavering, as if he was trying to read her reactions. "Katie, did you have to hide what he had done to you?"

A tear ran down her face. "He got me pregnant, but he wouldn't marry me. He was too far above me."

"*He* was too far above *you*?" Michael said with a raised eyebrow and a hint of irony in his voice.

"Yes. He wanted nothing to do with me when he found out about the child."

"And so you came to England to have your baby."

She almost begged him not to ask her anymore.

Michael hesitated, and then he held her face cupped in his hands, and leaned forward to kiss away the tears. "Tell me," he whispered.

"I don't talk about it. That's how I get by."

He was undaunted. "You risked living in London with all the bombing to keep it a secret?"

"I had no choice."

"Your family, your parents—they wouldn't help you?"

"I couldn't tell them."

"But didn't you want to tell your mother? If you had found the courage to tell her, maybe she would have understood."

"Not my mam. She didn't want to know, and my father would have beaten me black and blue."

He swore gently under his breath. "I see. So you had to tell people you were coming to England to do nursing," he said. "Or at least that's the tale I got from Marjory Mallory."

"Yes. But the first nursing I ever did was for you."

He smiled and gave her a kiss.

She sighed. "I found the address of a place that helps stupid girls like me, and I went there. It wasn't a nice place, but I was grateful. I stayed there until . . . " she knew that her voice was very shaky now.

"Until your child was born and given away?"

She couldn't answer him. She didn't want to say the words. Saying the words meant accepting the truth.

"I want to help get your baby back, Katie. I know you will have signed papers and you probably imagine all is lost, but with money and a really good lawyer—"

"No!" She stopped him, touching her hand to his mouth, shaking her head. The words he meant so kindly pierced her heart. "She was never adopted."

His eyes met hers, as he began to understand. "Something went wrong?"

"She was born too early, she was too little . . . "

"Oh, Katie," he gathered her back into his arms, and she sobbed freely now. He held her tight, and tried to offer her some comfort. "I wanted to stay, you know. I wanted to stay and hold your hand. And I could have—we were bombed in."

"Nobody thought less of you for going. I was just a stranger to you, sir."

"You needed me."

They were holding hands tightly now.

His blue eyes were full of heartfelt apology. "I don't know why I didn't stay. Fear, embarrassment, I suppose. Never seen a woman give birth before. Plenty of horses, of course, but never a woman."

"It doesn't matter, Michael."

"It does. I thought a lot about it afterwards, I wondered what had happened."

"It was awful. You were better off out of it."

"You were so scared—I could see the fear in your eyes. I ran away from it, and that was cowardly. I hated myself for it."

"She was born about three hours after you left. And she lived only an hour more."

"I wish I'd seen her."

His words gutted her with their sincerity, and Katie lost her heart in the pain of the memory. Tears came fast now, tumbling down her cheeks. "She tried to open her eyes, Michael, she tried.

She fell asleep in my arms. She looked like a little angel."

Michael wrapped his arms around her, and held her tight. "I'm so sorry. I thought it was the *man* you grieved for, not the child. If only I could give you another little girl," he said. He kissed her forehead and cradled her while she let out some of the grief she had held so close to her heart.

It was a few moments before it sunk in, what he had told her. She turned and looked up at him. "No kiddies, then, for you? No heir for all of this?"

"No." His voice sounded empty and hollow.

"It seems so unfair, that you should lose that hope along with everything else."

"Yes, it does," he said. But she noticed, for the first time, that he spoke of this loss with no anger, no rage, and no bitterness. They held each other for a long time, listening to their collective breathing. Finally, Michael turned her face toward his, and his blue eyes were very intense. "If you wanted to, Katie, we could comfort each other."

She didn't answer straight away. She stared back into his clear blue eyes and felt as if she knew at last why she was here, and what had brought them together. "Perhaps we could," she said. "I'll do anything you want."

He paused, gazing at her. In his eyes she saw hope, and longing, and tender compassion, but he didn't move. Finally he spoke, as if it wasn't easy to find the right words.

"You've been crying," he said. "It would be wrong of me to take advantage of you now. Go to sleep, my darling. But tomorrow morning, when we wake, I'll ask you again. If you still want to, we could try."

She let out a breath and her tension began to ease. It seemed right that they should wait, and she nestled against him, enjoying his warmth. He knew everything about her and he still held her and kissed her hair. For the first time in ages, it seemed easy to set all her troubles aside and drift away into sleep.

# Chapter Twenty-One

Michael lay awake for a long time, wondering if he'd said the right thing. He heard the clock striking midnight, and then he thought he heard it strike one, and after that he must have dozed off. He awoke with a start when he heard a noise downstairs. Maybe it was a rat. He'd have to speak to Jessop about it tomorrow morning. He lay awake, listening keenly, until he heard another distant crash. Someone had knocked something over. Something metal.

It sounded like an intruder.

Katie was in a deep sleep beside him, so he didn't wake her. He reached for his dressing gown and hauled it on, then maneuvered himself into his chair as quietly as he could, and went to investigate.

*

He wheeled himself quietly along the hall, becoming anxious when he saw the flicker of light under the kitchen door, until he heard the voices. Even before he pushed open the heavy oak door, he knew what he would find.

The children were in the kitchen. They had lighted two candles, which annoyed Michael, because candles were rationed, plus there was the danger of burning the house down. They were gathered around the table, tucking into bread and jam.

Michael flicked on the kitchen light and they all blinked at him in dismay. Alfie was standing on a stool over by the Aga, heating something in a small saucepan. He was so shocked to see Michael that he nearly lost his balance.

"What the dickens are you doing down here?" Michael shouted, hoping to put the fear of God into them. The twins practically jumped out of their skins.

Roy tried to be the spokesman for them all. "Having cocoa, Mister Lord. Want some?"

"No, I do not want cocoa at two o'clock in the morning. You can't come down here and help yourself to food and beverages in the middle of the night."

Bob started to cry, and by the looks of her, not for the first time.

George tried to intercede on behalf of his twin sister. "Don't be angry, Mister. Bob got nightmares, and we went to look for Miss Rafferty because she knows how to make the nightmares go away. Only she's gone, sir. Miss Rafferty's gone."

"She's not gone," Michael said with a bit of a hesitation. "She's asleep."

"She isn't," George told him, in tones of great anxiety. "She's not in her room, and it don't look like her bed's been touched since yesterday."

"We've searched the 'ole house, Mister Lord," Bob told him. "Top to bottom."

Michael glanced furtively at Alfie, to see if he had already worked it out.

Alfie was keeping very quiet, watching the milk boiling on the Aga, but when Michael caught his eye, he spoke. "George reckons she's run off back to London," he began cautiously, "but I thought we should wait and see if she turns up tomorrow."

"She didn't even say goodbye," Bob wailed. "And now we've got nobody to look after us. Only horrid old Jessop and she hates us!"

Michael knew he had to confess. "Look, Bob, there's no need for tears. Miss Rafferty hasn't gone anywhere. She's in my room."

"I told ya!" Roy said. "Didn't I say she was most likely warming up his bed?"

"Roy," Michael said, in a warning tone, but the boy's face was sullen and hostile.

"What? All night?" said George, incredulously. "She's been warming it up all night?"

"She's been giving him a bit of a cuddle, if you ask me," Roy said.

"Roy!" Michael expostulated.

"But I want her to give *me* a cuddle," Bob said, and burst into a fresh bout of wailing.

Alfie stared curiously at Michael. "What I can't work out," he began, "is why she'd even want to cuddle you, when you are so old and prickly."

"There's no accounting for taste," Michael said in an acid tone, but then he softened. "Roberta, come here, poppet. Don't cry."

Bob came forward rather shyly and then climbed onto Michael's lap, resting her tear-stained face on the satin lapel of his dressing gown.

Roy hadn't finished, his surly face was red with anger and his voice as gruff as he could make it for twelve years old. "Mrs. Jessop says it's a stupid girl that gets into the lord's bed."

"Does she indeed?" Michael said, experiencing a flare of anger at the thought of the old woman's interference. The little girl clung to him like a limpet. Michael sighed. "It's a bit different in my position, isn't it?"

"What position is that?" Roy said, with an ugly look on his face.

"Wash your mouth out, young man. If I had dared to utter such insolence to my father, Roy, he would have given me a hiding."

"Well, you ain't me dad, you're just some toff what fancies Rita Hayworth and Irish girls."

"We've had quite enough discussion of my private life. You can't come down here and crash around in the middle of the night, and you can't help yourself to all sorts of things out of the pantry. It's an outrageous abuse of my hospitality."

At that moment, the milk boiled over, causing complete chaos. Roy swore like a sailor, while Alfie tried to rescue the last little bit. The whole kitchen smelled of burnt milk and George suddenly acquired the look of a boy who had wet his pajamas. From a vantage point on Michael's lap, much too near to Michael's ear drums, Bob kept up a cat's chorus of hysterical wailing.

"Silence!" he roared. It was time to take control of this situation.

He sent Roy to bed, George to change, and Alfie was permitted to drink the last bit of boiled milk, cooled down with water. Then he was sent to bed as well.

Michael wheeled back up the hallway with Bob on his lap, promising her that nightmares would pass and Katie would make them all breakfast as usual tomorrow.

He hoped like hell that Katie would. This night wasn't over yet.

Bob lifted her little dark head. "Hey, Mister? Why did you tell Roy to wash his mouth out?"

"Because he was very cheeky."

"But, he didn't say a swear word. I was listening all the time and he didn't say one."

"Never mind, poppet, you'll understand when you're older. Now if you promise to be very quiet, I'll show you where Miss Rafferty is sleeping, and then you will know that she's here and you can see her tomorrow. You have to be very quiet, though . . . "

"I will be. Hey, Mister?"

"Yes?"

"I think Roy really likes Miss Rafferty, too."

"I know," Michael said, and wheeled off into the darkness. "And I have every sympathy with him, Bob. It's no damn good when somebody pinches your girl. I'll talk to him in the morning. I could offer him my picture of Rita Hayworth, of course, but it might only make things worse."

\*

He tried not to wake Katie as he eased himself back into bed. She looked so lovely in the half-light, the shape of her face, her shoulders, her arms, in the soft gray light that came in at the casement window.

So, everyone knew. And they thought the worst. Whatever the truth of it, Michael wanted her to wake up.

I'll do anything you want, she had said. He'd like to hold her to that promise.

# Chapter Twenty-Two

Katie woke up feeling warm and safe in Michael's arms. She loved that. He had such strong, muscular arms. She turned to look at him, and saw that he was already awake, waiting for her. He knew all her secrets, and he still wanted her—wanted her more than ever, in fact. He stroked her cheek.

She blushed when she thought of how their conversation had ended last night He said nothing at all, but he took her hand and placed it where she would feel that he was hard and firm.

Katie's voice shook when she spoke. "Would you like me to touch you?"

"Very much," he said, with a raised eyebrow that sent a shiver down her spine.

She peeled back the bedclothes, and there where his silk dressing gown had slipped apart during the night was his long, firm erection. She curled her fingers around him. She felt very self-conscious, and he didn't make it easy for her. He watched every move she made with a hint of a smile on his lips. She had no idea what he could feel. She touched him tentatively at first, as if she was afraid of hurting him.

He gave her a teasing grin. "It's not made of porcelain, you know."

She curled her hand around him, taking a good, firm hold, and did what she thought any man would enjoy.

"Am I doing it right, sir?" she said. "Can you feel it?"

Michael stroked the side of her face. He spoke in a sexy whisper. "Katie, given the degree of intimacy we're enjoying, do you think you could try out my first name?"

"Michael," she said, with a blush. It still sounded a bit submissive. "Michael. Michael," she tried it out until it sounded as if she had a right to say it, and she began a steady rhythm with her right hand.

"That's better," he said.

She didn't know which he liked— the way she said his name or the way she was touching him. Just now she was stroking the entire length of his erection and it grew even harder and firmer with every stroke. She couldn't look him in the eye, but she managed to bury her sense of shame in her determination to give him pleasure. "Can you feel that?"

"Maybe," he said in a teasing tone. "If you stroke a little faster, I might be able to tell you."

She obeyed.

He gave a sort of shivery sigh. "Mmm . . . I love watching you doing that."

"You're very hard now, that's for sure."

He placed a hand on hers to stop her, and suddenly he seemed agitated. "Katie, I'd like to flip you onto your back and go at it like crazy. Love you so hard you'll never want to love anyone else." He bit his lip and glanced away. "But I can't. I can't do any of that."

He composed himself and continued. "The only way we can do this is if you take the lead. Do you understand?"

"Yes, sir. I could try. If that's what you want."

"My name is Michael," he reminded her, patiently. "And I want you very much. More than anything in the world." He pulled her down onto his chest and stroked her hair. "I have come too far today to give up now."

He lifted her head and gave her long deep kisses until she began aching for him. But she still didn't "take the lead." Not yet.

"Take that dreadful thing off, darling," he said, in a low, suggestive, tone. He tugged at the front of her nightgown, daring her to take it off. "Looks like something they'd dish out in a Victorian workhouse."

She sat up, grasped the garment with both hands, and pulled it over her head.

"Oh, sweetheart!" He traced his fingers languidly over the

curve of one breast. He leaned forward and kissed it, carefully. He pushed her down and lay her back on his pillows, and then he went lower and lower, kissing her as he went, her breasts, her nipples, the curve just under her breasts, her smooth flat stomach. She could feel his breath on her skin as he went down until he found the place he really wanted to kiss. Somehow, she knew exactly what he would do, and how it would make her feel. She shivered with delight and fear.

"Michael," she whispered, as he moved his tongue in warm wet circles, making her long for whatever he could give. Sweet sensations sent her wild with desire. She surrendered to the feel of his tongue laving against her body, arousing her, exciting her, pushing her on toward the possibility of delicious pleasure. But then he stopped.

"Michael, please!" she murmured.

He lifted his head and spoke. "I could pleasure you like this," he said in a soft, seductive tone, "but wouldn't you like me inside you?" She knew that he longed to be inside her above all else. She was scared. She had no idea what it would involve or what he was capable of. But she longed to please him.

He continued to look deep in her eyes. How could she deny him? How could she deny herself? She hesitated. Burning with a mixture of desire and fear.

"Are you sure I won't get in the family way?" she said.

"I'm pretty sure," he said. There was so much regret in his voice that she wished she hadn't mentioned it, for his sake. It must be painful to be reminded of what he had lost, but heavens, she knew what it meant to bear a child out of wedlock and she couldn't go through that again.

"Look, Katie, you need to know the truth, if we're going to go ahead and do this. As you can see, I get aroused, just like any other man," he said, softly. "Especially with you in my arms. But . . . "

He hesitated, so she waited, patiently, until he was ready to tell her the rest.

He couldn't look into her eyes. He seemed to have to force himself to say the words out loud. "The doctors told me that I might still be able to give a woman pleasure as long as she takes the active role, but I am most unlikely to be able to father a child."

"Does that mean you won't . . . enjoy it?" Katie said.

"I used to think so. But looking at you now, all I keep thinking is how much I want to be inside you, even if I can't feel it in the same way. It would please me to please you, my darling, if you will only agree to try."

"I would do anything for you, you know that."

He smiled, and stroked her face. "Thank you. You'll be wonderful."

They changed places. He moved deftly to lay back on the pillows again, and she knelt beside him. She could feel her heart thumping at what she had promised to do. Her legs trembled as she moved gingerly until she was sitting astride him.

"You look fantastic from down here, you know." His hands went straight for her breasts.

Katie blushed to the roots of her hair. "You look good from up here, too."

He smiled. He wasted no time; he left her breasts and went lower, his long slender fingers slipping down between her thighs. He found the right place; he parted her gently and positioned the tip of his erection there between her legs. All she had to do was let her body slide down upon it, taking him inside, inch by inch.

She obeyed her instincts and lowered her body down to meet his.

She was completely unprepared for the sweet sensation that filled her as she let him in. "Michael! Oh, can you feel that?"

"Yes," he said, his voice rich with happiness. His blue eyes darkened with passion, now that they were coupled fully and completely.

Katie had no idea if he could really feel it in the same way that she did, or if he only felt it in his heart and in his mind. But her pleasure was so real and so strong that it was almost unbearable. He was guiding her with his hands, urging her to move, but she needed no guidance now. She rocked her body against his, and gave in to it. This feeling was too powerful to resist. Every move she made seemed to please him, and her confidence rose and swelled.

All sense of modesty was gone. She held onto his arms, her fingers digging into his biceps. Her hair streamed forward as she bucked her body against him again and again. Each thrust was slick and sweet because she was so wet. He moaned in pure delight, and she rode on into the arms of ecstasy.

"What can you feel, Michael?" she cried out.

"Your perfect body," he said. His hands roamed over her, hungry and desperate. "My God, Katie, come now. I want you to come now!"

So, she came crashing down, rippling against him, and their bodies joined together in one last frantic moment. He held her as if he would never let her go, and the feeling poured out over them both.

She was breathless from the exertion. The explosion of pleasure had been so intense, so exhilarating. But as it ebbed away, she was worried. She hoped she'd done it right. She hoped she hadn't hurt him, and that he wasn't shocked she had turned into a wild, crazy girl in his arms. She saw that his face was wet with tears, and a pang of love went straight through her. "Was that what you were expecting?"

"It was perfect." He pulled her close and shed more tears, long gasping sobs of relief.

Katie cradled him while he wept. She waited patiently, stroking his honey-gold hair, while he let go of everything he had lost and held tightly onto what he had found.

# Chapter Twenty-Three

All through breakfast, Michael couldn't help turning to look at her, wanting to take any opportunity to drink in the sight of her again. Her face was pink, and her long auburn curls were still wet from the bath. She looked exceptionally pretty, he thought, but he was bound to think that after what they had shared. She had been glorious this morning—all her hot, sweet curves pressed against him, her long hair tumbling down over her breasts, and her lips bending down to meet his.

This wonderful girl had given him the sweetest night of his whole life, but she was embarrassed about it, that much was clear. She seemed especially anxious not to meet Mrs. Jessop's eye. She turned away from the housekeeper to put the kettle on, and met Michael's eye instead. She colored up innocently as if she were still a modest little convent girl. She lowered her lashes, and ran her tongue over her lips to moisten them. Oh, when he thought of what she could do with those luscious lips of hers, and that tongue! Michael felt the familiar thrill of desire snaking through his body once more.

"Why do you keep staring at her, Mister Lord?" Bob wanted to know.

"Was I?" Michael replied, with mild surprise.

"Yes, you was," George confirmed.

"Somebody pass me the paper then," Michael suggested, "so I've got something to take my mind off Miss Rafferty."

"Mister Lord? Are you in love with Katie?" Alfie asked outright.

*Love.* Michael felt a strange pang when he heard the word and glanced up to see how Katie had reacted. She glanced down at her feet and her cheeks went even pinker than before. *They had made love, but were they in love?*

He adored her, but he had no right to claim her as his own. She deserved more than he could give. She loved children, he knew that, and sooner or later she would want to try for a family again. He wouldn't deny her that. Was that love?

Michael reached out and took her hand, refusing to let her pull away. He drew her nearer, to stand right beside him.

"Yes," he said, kissing the inside of her wrist, where her skin was very soft and sensitive. "Yes, I believe I am."

After a long, pregnant pause, two people got up and left the room. One of them was Mrs. Jessop and the other was Roy.

"Oh, sir," Katie said, "you're full of nonsense. Now look what you've done."

"Jessop's a prude," Michael said, "and Roy's still smarting because he's not old enough to woo you himself. They'll calm down eventually."

"We don't mind if you love Katie," Alfie said, acting as spokesman for the twins, who just kept staring from Katie to Michael and back again in curious amazement.

"This is not to be discussed in the school playground, do you understand me?" Katie said.

*

Later, when the children had gone to school, Katie laid out a tray of tea and delivered it to Michael's study, where he was working at his desk. He stopped what he was doing and kissed her hand.

"I think I should offer to adopt Roy," he said.

Katie couldn't quite believe she'd heard him right.

"I ought to adopt the boy. His Aunt Madge has sent me a rather unpleasant letter saying she doesn't want him back, and he hasn't any other family as far as we know. None willing or able to take him in and look after him properly."

"It's a kind thought, but this is Roy we're talking about. If it were Alfie or the twins, I'd understand. Bob adores you and George looks up to you. Alfie worms his way into everyone's heart. But Roy? Are you mad?"

"Probably," Michael agreed, ruefully. "But it's what needs to be done, Katie. Someone has to take responsibility for him. Where will he go after the war?"

"You aren't even old enough to be Roy's father," Katie murmured, as if it mattered.

"Katie, I am Roy's father—the only one he's ever had—and he takes notice of me now. He's even picking up my accent."

"They all are. Alfie's the worst. He sounds like a proper little toff, and Bob's getting a debutante's drawl. If this war goes on much longer we'll be sending them back to London sounding like the landed gentry."

"Roy won't be going back, if he agrees to this. He'll stay on here with me."

"Will he inherit?" Katie said curiously, the question out of her mouth before she could stop herself.

"I have no idea. I'll discuss it with my lawyer. That's not the point anyway. The boy needs stability."

They both paused for a moment. The very thought of surly old Roy taking Michael's place in the House of Lords one day was enough to boggle the mind.

Michael glanced up at her. "I wanted to ask you what you thought of the idea before I made the arrangements."

Katie knelt beside the wheelchair, and took Michael's hand. "I think you are the most kind-hearted, generous man I ever met," she said.

*

In the weeks that followed, they made love every chance they got. Sometimes when they were alone in his four-poster bed, they would join together side by side and he would kiss her neck and whisper words of love. He couldn't love her the way he wanted to, but she would rock her hips against him very gently, and he enjoyed watching her experiencing all the sweet sensations his body gave her.

Some nights that was all it took, especially if he slipped his hand down between their warm bodies to press the trigger, as he called it. Her climax was always long and vocal, and he reveled in it. Her sweet moans of womanly pleasure delighted him. He would let her cry out his name while he brushed away the tangle of red hair from her face and placed gentle kisses on her lips and cheeks.

Most of the time, though, she took the lead. She'd sit astride and drive him wild with her hot, sweet moves. He would lie back and enjoy the show. He loved watching her come again and again, enjoying the way her legs trembled when the passion was almost too much for her. She was like a butterfly, fluttering over nectar.

Since that first time together, he had come alive. The leaden heart he had carried around before was gone. He felt happy all day long, and nothing was a burden any more. He was up early every day, tackling the problems that dogged the farm, getting out into the fields to see the crops for himself, ordering Hammond around, and directing the action. He felt strong and useful again—after all, he was feeding Britain.

It was August, and he was busier than he had ever been with the harvest underway. He came in from the fields about four. He rolled his chair up the ramp that led directly into the kitchen and called out to her, but there was no reply.

"Katie! I'm home!"

There was silence.

She wasn't in the scullery. She wasn't in the corridor.

"What's for dinner, darling, I'm starving," he tried again. Michael realized he sounded like a husband, but he banished that thought.

That avenue was much too difficult to explore just at the moment.

"Where are you?"

He pushed open the door of the front reception room, the room they never used. And there she was, seated primly on one of the uncomfortable Louis the Fourteenth chairs.

"What the devil are you doing in here, darling?"

He rolled into the room, and all became clear. Katie was entertaining some unexpected visitors.

The man wore important-looking ecclesiastical robes. The nun wore a black gown with a white headdress and the second woman was dressed like every other middle-aged lady in wartime: A-line skirt, sensible short-sleeved blouse, large brown handbag, gas mask at her side. The visitors were drinking tea, and they looked very sour and very prim when Michael appeared.

"Michael, this is Monsignor Delaney," Katie explained, "Sister St. Paul, and Mrs. Bernadette Brown, who runs a home for fallen women."

*Holy cow!* Michael stared at the trio of people who had invaded his home with undisguised irritation. *Busybodies and troublemakers, and they are almost certain to upset Katie.* He suppressed the next blasphemous phrase that was on his lips, and uttered one word. "Charmed."

"We have been alerted to Miss Rafferty's situation by her mother," announced the Monsignor, placing his teacup down on its saucer with reverent care. "She has received troubling news from a Mr. Tom O'Brien, your lordship."

Michael's heart sank.

"It appears that her daughter's role here as nursemaid to four children has changed, and not for the better," said the Monsignor, gravely. "One might even go so far as to say that Katie's mortal soul is in danger."

Michael would have laughed if the mood in the room had not been so desperately somber. It was obvious Katie was mortified by the visit. The girl almost convulsed with shame when the Monsignor got out the letter and passed it across so that Michael could have a look.

"That letter isn't addressed to me," Michael said. "I was never intended to read it, so I'm not going to."

The three visitors all pursed their lips in unison.

Katie looked at him as if he were a canonized saint, and Michael handed the letter to her with a flourish.

There was a long, awkward pause before Mrs. Brown spoke. "We came to make one last appeal to Miss Rafferty, to beg her not to give in to your immoral requests. If she isn't able to go home to Ireland, we'd like her to come with us, and we'll find her a safe place to stay."

"And what does Katie say to that?" Michael enquired, with a certain amount of irritation in his voice.

"She hasn't given us her answer, yet."

"Did you realize, your lordship," the nun interrupted, "that Katie's parents have long entertained the hope that she might become a bride of Christ?"

Michael snorted, and then he grinned. "Katie *is* an angel," he began, innocently, "but I don't think she'll ever be a nun."

He just caught a hint of the smile Katie choked back when he glanced at her, but she managed to suppress it.

"Well, Katie?" Michael said. "Are you packing up that cardboard suitcase of yours and leaving me, darling?"

Katie moistened her lips, then said firmly, "No, sir."

"Well, in that case, we can bid our esteemed visitors good day. I hope you'll convey my respects to Katie's mother. Tell her that her daughter is in very good hands."

"Will I tell her that wedding bells will be heard before long?" said the Monsignor, with a sour look on his face.

"What?" said Michael.

Mrs. Brown took up the cudgels. "Look here. You've made it clear that you and Miss Rafferty have become . . . intimate. Are we to understand that you'll be making an honest woman of her?"

Michael bristled with annoyance. "That is a very impertinent question."

"It was a question that needed to be asked," added the Monsignor.

"No. It did not. Kindly leave my house before I get out of this chair and throw you out," Michael said, as if the force of his feelings would give him back the use of his legs at any moment.

Then he saw Katie's face, and instantly regretted his words. She looked saddened, disappointed even. She got up to show the visitors out and she kept her cool, but Michael knew she was hiding her feelings.

She must think he was acting like a complete cad. She knew nothing of the private agony he felt about their future. Katie deserved the best of everything. The very best. She'd make a fine wife, and a wonderful mother. Her strength of character and her determination were just what this place needed—what *he* needed. But how could he ask for that, when the partnership would be so unequal? When he couldn't give her children? For the first time in his life, Michael realized that for all his money and good fortune, he didn't really think he was good enough.

# Chapter Twenty-Four

Alfie would never have believed the boys' tales of a ghost if he hadn't woken up one night and heard it for himself.

He decided that this ghost business needed to be investigated.

First of all, he had to work out where the noise was coming from. When he had discovered that, he had a feeling that the rest of his scientific inquiry would fall into place.

He went down the curved stone steps that led downstairs. He crept past his lordship's bedroom, not wanting to wake him. He opened the double doors that led through the adjacent sitting room and into the Long Gallery, the huge long room where all the paintings were displayed. He was so small and light he could move without making a sound. He hid in the shadow of a defunct grandfather clock and peered along the gallery.

"Thump, thump, thump."

Now that he was nearer, he could hear another noise, a sort of rhythmic scraping noise, and something that sounded a bit like a door with a squeaky hinge.

"Oh, my giddy aunt," Alfie muttered under his breath as he peeked into the Long Gallery. It was Mister Lord, and he was *walking*—sort of. He had rigged a kind of walkway for himself between two rows of old wooden chairs, turned so that he could use the backs of the chairs for support. He was staggering along, very slowly, huffing and panting with the effort. His legs didn't bend like a normal person's legs; instead, they clanked. Alfie realized he must be wearing some kind of leg braces for support. Alfie thought they needed a little oil, because Mister Lord was squeaking like a rusty night. He kept his trap shut and watched to see what happened next.

When his lordship reached the end of the chair row, he hesitated uncertainly. He almost turned back and then decided to attempt a little unassisted walking. He took a few unsupported steps with a supreme effort. He wavered and wobbled dangerously as Alfie held his breath.

Michael tried to take the next uncertain step forward but his foot caught on the edge of the matting. Alfie wanted to close his eyes tight, but they remained wide open. Then, with all the grace of a tall pine tree being felled—and no one to call out "Timber!"—his lordship collapsed and fell heavily onto the stone floor of the Long Gallery.

He swore like a sailor, and rolled around on the floor trying to right himself for a while, while Alfie watched in horrified amazement. Alfie had two choices. He could run out from his hiding place to help, risking getting into trouble, or he could stay where he was and watch the poor man lying in pain on the floor.

He chose to give himself away. He ran forward and helped haul Michael into a sitting position.

Michael gave a start of surprise, and tried to push his assailant away. "What the devil—"

"It's not the devil, sir, it's Alfie."

"Yes, I can see that. What are you doing up and about?"

"I could ask you the same question, Mister. I don't think Katie would be too pleased if she knew you were doing something like this."

"You are not to tell her. I'm planning a surprise."

"She'll get a real surprise, all right, if she comes in here one morning and finds you in a heap on the carpet."

"I'd like to be able to ask her to dance," Michael said. "I'm getting better at it every night."

Alfie seriously doubted that Michael's staggering gait could ever be construed as dancing. He examined the leg braces critically. Michael straightened out his legs so the boy wonder could have a better look. The metal bars and struts formed a kind of supportive cage around each leg.

"Are they very heavy?"

"Very," Michael said, rubbing his legs ruefully.

"They need to be lighter," Alfie observed.

"I'm getting used to the weight every time I practice."

"Yes, but it's wearing you out. And it's putting you off balance, too."

Alfie examined the fastenings that went under each foot, attached with a little leather strap. "How did you get them on?"

"With great difficulty," Michael admitted. "Took nearly an hour the first time, I've got it down to about twenty minutes now."

Alfie suddenly had a light bulb moment. "I can see the problem. You're too tall."

"Nonsense, I'm exactly the right height."

"The braces aren't long enough then. They don't give you enough support."

Michael made a dismissive gesture with his hand. "Help me up, will you? I don't want to waste valuable time."

Alfie struggled to get Michael into a standing position.

"They aren't long enough, sir. You need to have some specially made."

Michael's face changed. Maybe he finally realized that Alfie might be right.

"Can you keep a secret, boy?"

Alfie nodded.

"If I took you to a place where they could make metal things, could you explain what you mean about making the struts longer?"

# Chapter Twenty-Five

Katie wrote a long letter to her mother, trying to undo some of the damage that Tom O'Brien had done. It was not the first time she had written home since the incident with the Monsignor. Her last letter didn't even get a reply. This time, she painted an elaborate picture of the whole situation between her and Michael, making it sound much more respectable than it was, telling her parents they mustn't worry, and that Tom was stirring up trouble, as always.

She felt a little guilty as she stuck the stamp on the envelope, but surely it wasn't a sin to pour oil on troubled waters?

Then she ran downstairs. In the hallway, she collared Roy to ask him to mail it for her. "See if you can catch the last post, there's a good boy. I'll give you a sixpence if you do."

"I'll do it for a shilling. It's a long walk down to the post office."

"Oh, it's not, Roy. For a big, strong lad like you, it's practically within shouting distance."

"Shilling. Or I'm not going."

"I'll take it myself if you're going to take that attitude. Only I've got the dinner to cook, and you do like bangers and mash, don't you Roy?"

"With gravy?"

"Lots of it. I might even do some onion rings if you take my letter down to the village."

Roy thought about this for a moment. "Where's the sixpence, then?"

Katie found it for him and told him to hurry. Then she retreated to the kitchen and set to work on the preparations for supper.

About two minutes later, she heard the unmistakable sound of a car engine. She looked up to see the MG, with Roy behind the wheel, rolling past the kitchen window.

"What in the blue blazes . . . " she murmured. She abandoned the sausages and ran out of the kitchen door.

"Roy! You can't! Stop. Wait."

She raced after the car as it disappeared round the side of the house.

"Stop right there, young man!"

She only caught up with him because he had to stop to open the front gate. She arrived beside the car, breathless and cross.

"What on earth do you think you're doing?"

Roy looked up at her like butter wouldn't melt in his mouth. "You told me to hurry. I was only trying to do what you said."

"I didn't say you could take his lordship's car."

Then Roy leaned across and opened the passenger door for her. Impersonating Michael's accent, he patted the seat and said, "Come on. Come for a spin. You know you want to."

Katie stared right back at him, unimpressed.

"Roy. For the last time. Stop that nonsense and get out of the car."

"What? And leave it here, blocking the gate? Come on Katie, it would only take a minute to whiz down to the post office and back. Don't be a spoil sport."

Katie sighed. "I've the dinner to cook."

"We could've been there and back in the time we've spent arguing about it," Roy pointed out. "Come on. We'll be back in two shakes of a lamb's tail. Honest!"

"I . . . suppose so," Katie said, not wanting to give in to the boy's demands, but keen to resolve the dispute somehow. "You'll have to let me drive."

"No. I'm not letting a girl walk all over me." Roy scowled at her.

Katie scowled back. "Then you'll be walking to the village, and getting no pocket money for a month."

She thought she was going to get another of his cheeky remarks, but after a few seconds, he seemed to recognize that a compromise was needed. Reluctantly, he relinquished the driver's seat and went round to the other side.

They got in the car and Kate jerked it backwards by mistake, and then ground the gears struggling to find the right one, before finally lurching into first and moving forward.

"Are you sure you don't want me to drive? I'm much better at it than you."

"Keep quiet and think about how you are going to explain this to his lordship when you get home, Roy."

Kate headed for the road that led down to the village, thinking what an obstinate young man Roy was for persuading her into this. Twisting country lanes were difficult to navigate at the best of times, but in this state of agitation—Kate wrestled with a bend in the road and the wheels squealed.

Roy seemed nervous. "Steady on! Or pull over and I'll drive."

"You will not. If I've told you once, I've told you a thousand times—"

"Look out!"

Kate tried to take the next curve, and this time, the car didn't make it. Kate lost control and the car squealed like an animal in pain. She saw Roy reach out and try to clutch at the steering wheel to help her, but it didn't work. She could hear someone screaming as the car left the road—a high-pitched scream of dismay—and only dimly registered that it was her own voice.

\*

Everything was eerily quiet, except for the hissing of the car, when Roy opened his eyes. The crash impact must have knocked him out for a few moments. He hoped it was only moments. He craned his neck and tried to see over the bonnet. The car must have careered off the edge of the road and down into the ditch. It was completely still now, nose down in the little stream of water at the bottom of the ditch. The windscreen was shattered and when Roy tried to move, he heard little bits of glass tinkling all around him. There was a smell of petrol and that peculiar hissing noise.

He turned awkwardly and glanced across at the passenger seat, fearful of what he might see. Katie was lying on her side, with her face away from him.

"You all right?"

She didn't answer, not even when he shook her. He didn't know how to take a pulse.

With a blind panic rising in his chest, he tried to get himself out of the car. The door was jammed but he slithered up and out of the window. He ran round the other side to see what had happened to Katie. Her eyes were closed.

Roy ran like the wind, only vaguely aware of an ugly looking gash on his arm. He felt no pain. He just kept running, feet slamming along the road in a rapid rhythm.

*Katie's hurt. The car's wrecked. Got to get help.*

At first, the fear and the adrenalin kept him running, but he was getting a pain in his side from running too fast. He didn't even consider the possibility that another car might come along in the opposite direction. It hardly ever did. He had to find a house and there wasn't one anywhere in sight. He hoped he didn't have to run all the way back to Great Farrenden to get help. He'd just about die if he had to do that.

Then, Roy saw a small row of cottages, and with a new burst of energy, he sprinted toward the first one. He almost keeled over in the front porch, so out of breath he was unable to knock on the door. But they must have seen him coming, because the door opened, and a lady in hair rollers appeared.

"Help me, please," gasped Roy. "There's been an accident. She's hurt."

"Your mother?"

"No. Not my mum, my mum's dead. No, Katie's not dead. I hope not, but she wasn't moving. You've got to help her!"

\*

Katie woke to find herself on the chaise in the library. Michael had been banished from the room, and she was alone with Dr. Larchwood.

"Steady on," he said, when she tried to hoist herself up into a sitting position. "You fainted, my dear, from the shock of the car accident. Do you remember?"

Visions of coming to in the car flooded into Katie's mind.

"Yes, I remember. Oh doctor—I've wrecked his lordship's MG. He loved that car."

"I'm more concerned about you. Lie back on the couch for a moment, there's a good girl."

He examined her carefully, flexing each of her limbs to check to see if anything was broken, examining her cuts and bruises.

"Blood pressure seems fine, so probably no internal bleeding," he murmured to himself. "I'm just going to palpate your tummy a bit to make sure you didn't sustain internal damage."

He pressed gently here and there. Then more firmly—experienced hands moving across her belly. His face became suspicious. He pressed down hard while Katie frowned in confusion. A doctor had done that to her once before.

"You have a boyfriend," he said, as if he was stating a fact.

"No," said Katie. "I don't." She could hardly tell Dr. Larchwood about Michael.

In an instant, Katie guessed the reason for his accusation "I couldn't be! He swore it wasn't possible!"

# Chapter Twenty-Six

Dr. Larchwood was surprised to find Michael was waiting to ambush him in the hall. The wheelchair was parked by the front door and it was obvious his lordship would not let him pass until he knew the truth.

"What's the situation, then?" Michael asked.

Dr. Larchwood had heard the gossip in the village, of course, but he didn't believe it. He was a medical man, and he knew the extent of Lord Farrenden's injuries. Katie must have a fellow in the village, some lusty young man from Market Farrenden would be responsible for this. The men hadn't *all* been called up yet.

"A few cuts and bruises, from which she will make a complete recovery," Dr. Larchwood said, with a bit of a smirk on his face. He wasn't sure if he should mention the other matter just yet, though it would be plain to everyone soon. Then, his young lordship would have to dismiss his pretty serving wench and find another.

"Is there something else wrong with her?" Michael asked impatiently. "I've been very worried."

Dr. Larchwood abandoned Katie's confidence lightly, like shrugging off a waistcoat in the heat. "She's pregnant," he said, in a matter-of-fact tone.

"She's pregnant?" Michael's blue eyes went wide.

Dr. Larchwood was more than a little surprised by the look on Michael's face, for it was the same astonished but pleased look that many an expectant father had given him when he had delivered the happy news.

"Yes. Most definitely pregnant, and she'll be fine. She's a strong young woman and most likely she'll have a bouncing healthy baby next spring."

His lordship's face was a picture. It flickered from one emotion to the next passing through disbelief, pride, and anxiety all in a matter of seconds.

Dr. Larchwood chuckled. "If you'll forgive my curiosity, my lord, how the devil did you manage that?"

Then he braced himself for an outburst of aristocratic rage. He hadn't been able to resist asking the question, but Michael would be certain to deny it.

Instead, a delicate flush of color began to rise on his lordship's face, and he didn't reply. So, the rumors were obviously true. The angry young man in the chair had a pretty Irish sweetheart, and she was having Michael's child. The village would go wild when this got out.

Michael spoke in a measured tone. "You may send me your bill, Doctor, and I will settle it with my monthly accounts. Would you mind showing yourself out, if you please? I must go and see Katie."

*

She was lying on the couch in front of the fire with an old eiderdown over her. She looked up at him when he came near.

"You lied to me," she said. She looked pale and vulnerable, and she shivered under the eiderdown. She was still a little shaky from her accident.

Michael took her hand, and kissed her fingers. "I've been an idiot," he admitted. "But I swear I never meant to hurt you. They told me it wasn't possible. I believed them."

"And I believed you," she said ruefully.

"Yes." He wasn't sure if he should add that he was sorry, but it didn't seem altogether true, so he didn't. He supposed he should feel a sense of guilt, but it simply wasn't there. Instead, he felt a surge of excitement at being alive. He could father a child!

"You're not sorry," she said.

"Of course, I'm sorry," he lied. "I should have realized the doctors could be wrong."

"You've let this terrible thing happen to me all over again, and it will be worse than before, for I had no feelings at all for him, though I cried a thousand tears when my daughter died." She began to sob heavily.

"Katie, it'll be different this time. I swear to you and you must believe me now, because this is the truth. We will face this together. You must let me take care of you, as you have taken care of me. Give me a little time, my love, and I promise I will make everything right."

\*

In the village, the gossip went wild.

Katie found that out when she went down to the shops to buy the meat. She could hear what they were saying as she joined the queue.

"It couldn't be his of course . . . well, they can't, can they? Not with a broken back."

Katie knew her face was scarlet. She checked the contents of her basket just for somewhere to look.

"She can hear you, I think . . . "

"I feel a bit sorry for her . . . "

"She'll never get away with it . . . he'll know it couldn't be his. She'll get the sack, surely . . . "

Katie was mortified. These women didn't care that she could hear. They kept saying they were *so* sorry for her, but they didn't mean a word of it. They were obviously rather pleased that this disaster had befallen her. Katie fumed inside as she inched nearer and nearer the head of the queue. Apparently, her misfortune at getting pregnant out of wedlock helped make them all look upright and respectable by virtue of the comparison.

Katie was just some slattern from Ireland who had gone and made a fool of herself. Again.

She couldn't even walk off in disgust. They had nothing for supper and she was starving—the child inside her was already making demands on her body. So she had to stand there and listen to it all.

It had been more than a week since she and Michael had received the news. She dreaded the thought of another pregnancy. She didn't know how to face the long wait, the pain and the heartache, not knowing if this child would live, either. And although Michael had said that things would be different, nothing had changed. He had made her no promises and no offers. She began to fear it was all turning out like last time, when Tom and his parents had sent her packing, alone.

The unkind gossiping continued.

"What was that book—*Lady Chatterley's Lover*? I think that's the one. He was in a wheelchair, wasn't he? And she had an affair. Do they even *have* a gamekeeper at Farrenden Manor?"

Katie almost cried in fury and annoyance, and she was in tears by the time she reached the head of the queue.

The butcher's boy rested his hands on the counter and gave her an undisguised leer. "Well, Miss, what do you think his lordship might fancy?"

"Not you as well," she said, swiping away hot angry tears before she could hand over her ration books.

He gave a bit of a laugh. "If you think that's bad, you should hear what they're saying about you in the pub!"

*

Michael could see Katie was upset when she returned. She ran upstairs and wouldn't come down no matter how much he coaxed or demanded. It was Roy who clued him in.

"Fetch the car," Michael demanded. "The Austin. I'm going to sort this out, once and for all."

"Get my crutches out of my wardrobe and put them on the back seat."

Roy frowned, but he did as he was told. He owed Michael a huge favor for overlooking the wrecked MG.

"Go and get Alfie. Tell him we're going ahead with Plan A."

"What?"

"Just do it."

*

They drove without a word to the Dog and Whistle.

Michael had always imagined himself striding into the pub like a returning crusader after the war. Today, with Roy's help, he staggered across the forecourt upright, but only just. He more like lurched in, bit by bit on his crutches, legs braced.

Michael's face was fierce with determination. His hands gripped the crutches so tightly that his knuckles were white with the effort.

He may not have had the demeanor of a returning knight, but he silenced the room as he came through the low door of the Dog and Whistle. The laughter and the banter died and even the hardened drinkers and the men playing darts turned to stare. Some murmured "Yer lordship," and touched their hands to their foreheads as a mark of respect. But the words on most people's lips were plain and simple, and uttered in tones of deepest amazement.

*"He's walking!"*

The landlord of the pub hurried from behind the bar. "Your lordship! This is a most unexpected pleasure. Can I get you a drink, sir? And a seat by the fire?"

Two or three men instantly vacated the chairs by the fireplace, where a cheerful blaze burned merrily in the grate.

Michael dismissed him. "Not yet, man, no." He looked around the room, scanning the faces of local people he had not seen in months. He spoke in a loud, clear voice. "I understand that some extraordinary rumors have been going around about me."

There was a stunned silence.

"Apparently I'm a fool, conned by one of my own servants."

No one made a sound, the pub a sea of scared faces, frowning with confusion and surprise.

"A girl gets pregnant by one of you men, perhaps, and I am duped into believing the child is mine!"

Michael almost made the mistake of lifting up one of his crutches to wave it angrily at everyone, but he remembered to refrain in the nick of time. "I'm here today to set the record straight."

Some of them looked at him like guilty dogs while others gazed into the depths of their beer mugs.

"Do you imagine that I don't know what is required to get a girl pregnant?" Michael expostulated. There was a sort of splutter of suppressed laughter from one or two of the younger ones, but a nudge and a word of warning was all it took to restore the respectful silence.

Michael gripped his crutches even more tightly, willing himself to stay upright. "And you think the war has robbed me of the ability to do so?"

A low murmur circled the room.

"You are wrong," Michael bellowed. "Katie is carrying *my* child, and there is no question about it. You think I would *ever* allow any of you to touch the woman I have chosen for myself?"

"No, sir. Of course not." It was the publican who spoke up, desperate to pour oil on troubled waters. "Don't upset yourself, now, me lord. The boys were only concerned for you, because we heard you came back from the war with a broken back."

"Yes," Michael confirmed more quietly. "But even the worst wounds heal to some extent, as you can see." He noticed a shadow from the open doorway, and he turned to look. Katie stood there, behind him, listening to every word.

She must have run down from the house just after she saw him leaving with Roy in the Austin. She looked as stunned as everyone else in the room. Her face was white with shock. Michael gave her what he hoped was a warm smile of encouragement. Then he turned back to the crowd.

"She was purity itself when she came to work for me. So, I can only assume that the scurrilous rumors concerning Katie's reputation have been spread by those whose attempts to court her were less successful than my own. She is mine now. You people slandering her now, listen to me! You will never speak about my wife like that again."

There was a bit of a gasp.

"Yes. I said *my wife* because she is my wife, in every sense but one, and if I am lucky, she will agree to become my legal wife, and you will all bear witness to it."

Michael turned to her again. He wanted to stretch out his hand, invite her to come to him, but he couldn't. He dared not loosen his grip on the crutches even for a moment.

She approached him, eyes wide and fearful, shaking from the shock of seeing him on his feet. Her sweet face tilted up to him, her expression full of concern. He wanted to hold her, but he pressed on with what he had to say.

"Reach into my jacket pocket, my love," he invited her.

She did as she was told, and pulled out a letter with familiar handwriting.

"It's from my parents," she said in astonishment.

"Yes. I asked their permission for us to marry," he explained, in a voice loud enough for all to hear. "This has been the only reason for the delay, you understand. I hold you in the highest regard, and my devotion to you grows stronger every day. Now that I have their blessing, I can ask you to become my wife. I love you, Katie, please, will you be my lady?"

He watched her eyes go wide as she considered the implications. *Lady Farrenden.* Then her lips parted, but no sound came out from between them. She seemed to be as terrified as she did the first day she saw him. He wanted to take her in his arms and kiss her fears away, but he had to content himself with words.

"Katie, darling, I can't possibly kneel, and I rather doubt that I can stand for much longer," Michael said, shaking with the effort. "So *please*, put us all out of our misery and say yes," he said.

She took one last glance at her parents' signature on the letter in her hands, as if she could hardly believe they would allow it.

She nodded. "Yes," she stammered, "I'll have to marry you, won't I?" Then she burst into tears and smiles at the same time and flung her arms around his neck.

He nearly toppled off his crutches, but he managed to get his balance. "Steady on," he said, and smiled triumphantly at her and everyone else in the room. "Now, we shall require a round of drinks for everyone in the house, for I am *sure* that the whole room will want to raise a glass to our future happiness. Where is that chair by the fire?"

"We are delighted to bear witness to your recovery, sir," the landlord said, helping Michael across the room.

At last, a cheer went round the room, and people began to relax. People clapped Michael on the back, wished him health, wealth and happiness. People introduced themselves to Katie and spoke to her in a polite, deferential way that she'd never experienced in her life. Nobody was rude enough to mention the baby on its way.

Michael collapsed into a chair, clanking like a knight in rusty armor. The leg braces were desperately uncomfortable, so Roy ran forward to help him to release the catches so Michael could relax. Katie leaned forward and looked curiously at his ankles.

"I've been practicing for weeks," Michael confessed. "It was meant to be a surprise for our wedding day."

She smiled and fought back tears. "So you're the Ghost of Farrenden Manor," she said, with a hint of a smile.

"Yes, I was a ghost: a shadow of a man and a ghost of my former self. Until you came along. You breathed life into me, Katie. I wanted to surprise you."

"Oh, Michael, you did! It was wonderful. But, Michael, you didn't have to do this. I would have married you most willingly sitting down."

Michael caught her eye and raised his beer glass. "To us," he said quietly.

She heard him, despite the noise. "To us," she said.

# About the Author

Cody Young was born near Southampton, England, but now lives in New Zealand with her Italian husband and their three sons. She started writing historical romances in 2009, with another wartime story called *American Smile*. For more information about Cody, check out *http://codyyoungblog.blogspot.co.nz/* or *http://www.facebook.com/CodyYoungAuthor*.

In the mood for more Crimson Romance? Check out *Stubborn Hearts* by Carol Ritten Smith at *CrimsonRomance.com*.